SWEET FEROCITY

A DARK MAFIA ROMANCE

ZOE BLAKE

Copyright © 2022 by Stormy Night Publications and Zoe Blake
All rights reserved. No part of this book may be reproduced or
transmitted in any form or by any means, electronic or mechanical,
including photocopying, recording, or by any information storage and
retrieval system, without permission in writing from the publisher.
Published by Stormy Night Publications and Design, LLC.
www.StormyNightPublications.com
Blake, Zoe
Sweet Ferocity
Cover Design by Dark City Designs
Photographer: Wander Aquilar

This book is intended for *adults only*. Spanking and other sexual
activities represented in this book are fantasies only, intended for adults.

CHAPTER 1

atie
Worthington University, Virginia

IF I HAD KNOWN I was going to be kidnapped...

HE HAD LOOKED out of place, that was all I remembered.

I'd passed him on my way to the photography darkroom. On a college campus filled with students wearing shorts and hoodies in the middle of winter, the Japanese man in a long black leather trench coat calmly sitting on a park bench had stood out. He'd had on a pair of reflective sunglasses covering the upper part of his long, pale face and slicked-back, coal-black hair.

It had been the leather gloves that had seemed particularly odd to me.

I couldn't put my finger on why. They just did.

As I passed him, I had the distinct suspicion he was

watching me to the exclusion of all the other students scurrying past, which was crazy. Everyone on campus knew me as Katie Antonova. I'd used my mother's maiden name on my application. There was no reason why anyone would figure out I was the daughter of the notorious Russian crime boss Egor Novikoff, or the sister of my even more infamous brothers, Lenin and Leonid. I had buried that life in my past and that was where it was going to stay.

Shaking off the odd feeling, I ducked under a low tree branch and headed toward the two-story brick building that housed the art and culture classes on my campus. Stopping at the bulletin board to see if the test scores for my *History of Photography Through Art* class were posted, I then headed down the linoleum-covered staircase to the basement. While the upper floors housed dance and art studios, the basement was where they kept the pottery wheels, glazing kilns, and photography darkrooms.

This late in the day, I would have the place to myself. I clicked the lights on, squinting when the garish fluorescent lights flicked on one by one, until the entire basement was illuminated. I placed my shortyLOVE blue camo cross-body bag on the table and pulled out my favorite manual Pentax K1000 SLR camera and my hot-pink binder of film negatives, leaving my other favorite digital camera tucked inside my bag.

Tonight I was working with black-and-white film, so I was pretty excited to experiment with different exposure times to get just the right effect. After entering the darkroom, I turned on the overhead light and fan, then put on a pair of safety goggles and gloves as I got ready to mix my chemicals. Setting out my three trays, I prepared the developer, stop bath, and fixer. I then grabbed my pink binder and selected a row of negative film. Placing it on the lightbox, I tossed off my goggles and gloves and grabbed a loupe. I leaned down to examine each photo in detail.

Using a red grease pencil, I marked which photos I wanted to make into black-and-white prints. I placed the strip into the negative carrier and isolated one of the photos before raising and lowering the enlarger head to get the projected image to just the right size on the paper. I then used the focusing wheel to sharpen the image. After setting the aperture and my filter, I grabbed the timer. My plan for my test print was to divide the photo into three sections and expose each section by an additional five seconds.

Leaning over, I flicked off the white light and turned on the muted red one. I set my timer and began my test strip. After the allotted time, I used the rubber-tipped tongs to remove the paper from the developer and place it in the stop bath, then the fixer.

As I turned to clip the wet paper to the clothesline we had stretched across the darkroom, I heard a sound outside the darkroom door.

I paused to listen.

Nothing.

No out of the ordinary sounds.

A nervous chill ran up my spine.

Still, I tried to concentrate on my test strip. Each section was darker than the last. I decided the ten-second exposure was definitely going to be the best for this particular project. I turned to grab a fresh piece of photo paper when I heard it again.

It almost sounded as if someone was opening and closing each of the darkroom doors.

There were ten darkrooms lined up along the right wall of the basement.

Door number five. Click.

Door number six. Click.

Door number seven. Click.

Whoever it was, they were getting closer.

I was in the last one, door number ten.

Feeling silly for doing so, I reached over and turned the lock on the doorknob.

It was probably just a security guard checking to see if students were still in the building and nothing more.

Once again, I shook off the strange feeling and focused back on my project. This was due in class tomorrow, so I didn't have time to be messing around or giving in to nerves. I made a slight adjustment to the enlarger head and set my timer.

That was when the doorknob turned.

The air seized in my lungs as I pivoted my head to stare at it.

I prayed it was my imagination.

Unable to breathe, I waited.

It turned again.

The movement was slight and slow.

Methodical.

If it were just a security guard checking the doors, they would have rattled it more decisively. No, this was the action of someone who didn't want the person inside to know they were trying to open the door.

There was a long pause.

Then a soft, metallic scrape.

Then another.

I hadn't spent my early childhood surrounded by some of the most devious criminal masterminds on the East Coast without learning a thing or two. When I was as young as six, I'd had cousins teaching me how to pick a lock. I knew the sound like I knew my own heartbeat.

Another scrape.

Knowing it was pointless, I scanned the small darkroom. There was no other exit. The room was basically a closet with a waist-high counter around its perimeter and a narrow aisle down the center.

I was trapped.

My fingers gripped the edge of the counter as I fixated on the doorknob.

I jumped a foot when my ten-second timer went off.

I slammed my palm down on the timer, shutting it off.

The scraping at the door stopped.

I waited.

Nothing.

Using the counter because I didn't trust my quivering legs, I carefully stepped toward the door. Holding my breath, I leaned over and placed my ear against it and listened. There was the sound of fabric rustling.

Then another soft metallic scrape.

I covered my mouth to suppress a scream and backed away from the door.

Please God, let me be overreacting.

Let this be a phantom of my past tainting my new reality.

Just because I had been raised to see demons in the shadows didn't make it so.

What was that saying? The sound of horse's hooves didn't mean zebras.

Please God, don't let this be a fucking zebra.

The moment I heard the decisive click my body quaked.

Whoever it was, they had unlocked the door.

Once again, the doorknob slowly turned.

The door opened.

No light poured in.

The person must have turned off the basement fluorescent lights. Another really bad sign.

There was just the dark outline of a tall, slender person, but I knew immediately who it was.

It was the man from the park bench. The one wearing the gloves and leather trench coat.

Trying to throw the intruder off, I called out in French, *"Qu'est-ce que vous voulez?"*

Maybe I would get lucky, and the person wouldn't expect a supposed Russian mafia princess to speak French.

The man chuckled. "I know it is you, Katia."

Katia. Only people who knew the Novikoffs knew my true name was Katia, not Katie.

I backed up as far as the counter would allow. "What do you want?"

His voice was smooth and calm as if each word was cautiously spoken. "Why don't we speak outside?"

I shook my head. "I have nothing to do with my family's business and I don't know who you are."

He bowed his head slightly. "How remiss of me. My name is Kiyoshi Tanaka. I am… a business associate of your family."

I let out a shaky breath. "Well, as I said, I have nothing to do with my family or their business so you can have nothing to say that would interest me. So get the fuck out of my darkroom."

He took a step inside the small space. "There is no reason why we cannot be civil to one another. Your family has something I want. *You* are going to help me get it. I promise, if you cooperate, no harm will come to you."

I didn't believe him for a second.

I inched my hand toward the tray of chemical developer. "My bodyguard will be back at any moment. He will break you in half if he finds you here."

The man shook his head. "Tsk tsk tsk. You are a liar, my dear Katia. We both know your family does not care enough about your well-being to guard you. That is their mistake, and my good fortune."

The truth of his words stung.

Still, I had to try to talk my way out of this. It was my only defense. "If that is true then I can have no value to you."

Kiyoshi shrugged. "Sometimes the greatest treasures are the ones we miss only when they are gone."

"I'm not going anywhere with you."

"I do not wish to make this painful for you… but I will if I have to."

"I'll scream. The security guard will hear me."

Kiyoshi seemed unfazed by my threat. "The security guard is unfortunately no longer in a position to assist you."

Which meant he had either hurt the poor guard or outright killed him; either way, this had gone from bad to worse.

He took another step closer.

I was out of options.

In one fluid movement, I slipped my fingers under the tray of chemical developer and flipped it over, sending the chemical cascading down the front of Kiyoshi. He screamed as the chemical hit his eyes and mouth. The developer was heavily diluted and more dangerous to inhale than when exposed to the skin, but it would cause a slight chemical burn if it got in his eyes. Hopefully it would be enough to slow him down.

Shoving him aside, I raced out of the darkroom. Snatching my bag as I passed the table, I dove up the stairs. I had a lead of only a few strides before I heard Kiyoshi in pursuit.

I burst through the outer door. As I inhaled a deep breath of frigid air, getting ready to scream, a hard weight slammed into my back. I was forced to the ground off to the side by the bushes. A hand wrenched me to my feet by my hair. I clawed and scratched but didn't hit skin because of his leather gloves and coat.

A sweet-smelling cloth was placed over my nose and mouth.

Chloroform.

Fuck.

As my eyelids drooped and my knees buckled, I gave

up my fight and scrambled to reach into my cross-body bag. Knowing my attacker's vision would still be compromised, I grabbed my camera and lifted it over my shoulder and took as many photos as I could. I then tossed the camera into the bushes before everything went black.

If the bastard was going to kill me, at least my final justice would be one of my photos damning him to hell for it.

CHAPTER 2

*L*uka
Krasnoyarsk Prison Camp, Siberia

THIN-SOLED boots stomped into the muddy ground as the shouts and calls from the prisoners escalated. A sea of gray jumpsuits and shaved heads stretched around the bare exercise yard. Some clanked the tin mugs used for their daily allotment of weak soup and bread against the metal fence as they called out for the fight to begin.

I took it all in calmly through the smudged and barred window of my cell as I sipped my lukewarm tea. The rock walls were covered in a slimy layer of ice and grime that trickled down over my straw mattress. An emaciated rat scrambled from a hole, desperate for food. I tossed him the last piece of crust from my bread before rising. Shrugging out of the top of my jumpsuit, baring my chest, I wrapped the sleeves around my waist and made my way out to the yard.

A cacophony of screams and boot stomping greeted my entrance.

I pumped my fists and jogged in place, warming up my body as I surveyed the crowd, looking for my quarry. In a corner, I zeroed in on my target who was surrounded by prisoners bearing Nazi insignia. At six five and one hundred and fifty kilos I was an impressive size, but my opponent was bigger. Although a few inches shorter, his frame was bulkier with a significant amount of fat.

It would be an even fight.

I was still going to kill him.

Pieces of shit racists got on my nerves. Plus there was very little entertainment in a Siberian prison camp in the middle of winter.

A nearby prisoner placed two fingers in his mouth and a high-pitched whistle pierced the shouts of the crowd.

I slammed a fist into my palm and stalked forward. These were my favorite kinds of fights. Bare-knuckle, no-holds-barred. Winner was the man left breathing.

The man approached and opened his mouth wide to release what I assumed was supposed to be an intimidating roar. His rotted teeth and tobacco-blackened tongue were repugnant. Leaning back, I kicked his jaw shut. The man's head snapped back as he toppled to the ground. He rolled onto his side and spit out a mouthful of blood and a few teeth. The crowd swelled forward but was held back by several prisoners with their arms outstretched.

First rule of a prison fight. No interfering.

The man hobbled to his feet and raised his fists. "I'm going to kill you for that, Siderov."

"You can try, Olga," I said, using the female version of his name, Oleg.

The man cried out and charged. He swung his right arm wide, then the left. As he stretched his arm back for another swing, I kicked him square in the balls.

The man fell to his knees, grabbing his groin.

Second rule of prison fighting. Spare your knuckles.

I kicked him again in the jaw. This time I heard the bone crack as the lower part of his face hung slack.

He fell face-first into the mud.

Two of his compatriots surged forward. A few of the prisoners tried to hold them back, but I gave them a nod. The two men approached me.

Now I was finally going to have some real fun.

Stretching out my arms, I motioned with my fingers. "Bring it."

The men attacked.

I pounded the first in the left eye socket and then turned to send the second man flying backward with an uppercut to the jaw. The first approached again. As he swung high, I bent low and nailed him in the kidneys before slamming my open palm just under his ribcage, collapsing his lung. The man's eyes bulged as he staggered and fell into the waiting arms of the crowd.

The second man had a swastika tattooed on the front of his neck. I saw it as the perfect target. I grabbed him by the shoulder and held him in place as I ruthlessly pounded him in the throat. The man clutched and clawed at my arms as he struggled to breathe. He coughed and a fine mist of blood hit me in the face. Finally, I released him. He clutched at his throat as he fell to his knees.

The other prisoners surged forward. Several of them raised my arms in victory just as the guards' whistles blew and several shots were fired into the air, breaking up the fight.

I accepted the grimy towel offered and wiped the blood off my face before untying the sleeves of my prison-issued jumpsuit. I was pushing my second arm into a sleeve when one of the guards approached.

The guard motioned over his shoulder with his thumb. "Luka, you have a visitor."

I nodded as I buttoned the jumpsuit closed. "Where?"

"Boss says you can use his office."

I nodded again as I followed the guard out of the exercise yard. Prison was no different than regular society, just more violent. Just as in the real world, money bought privileges and obscene amounts of money, as I had, bought access to the prison chief's personal office.

Right before entering the office, I used the guard's sleeve to wipe the rest of the blood off my face. He sneered but did nothing. I opened the door.

Sitting in the high-backed leather chair of the prison chief was Egor Novikoff.

"Out of my chair," I ordered as I rounded the desk.

The two bodyguards he had brought with him stepped forward. The old man waved them off and dutifully switched to one of the more uncomfortable wooden chairs across from the desk.

I sat in the desk chair and reached across the desk to flip open the polished cigar box that rested on the corner. Selecting one, I bit off the end and reached into my pocket for my solid silver lighter. Holding the flame just below the tobacco so as not to burn it, I slowly lit the cigar, uncaring of the impatient looks Egor was sending me. When the cigar end glowed a bright orange, I leaned back in the leather chair and placed my muddy boots on the desk.

"To what do I owe the pleasure, Egor?"

"I need your help."

I shrugged. "Not interested."

"I'll pay. Big."

I took a long drag off my cigar. "Doubt you'll pay more than what this oligarch is paying me to watch over his son while he enjoys our mother country's hospitality."

One of the perks of being a mafia mercenary was I owed loyalty only to myself. Each of the syndicates had used my services at one point or another, but I didn't come cheap. A simple assignment would cost millions of American dollars, and nothing was beyond my skill set: assassinations, theft, arms deals. Hell, I'd even helped train a small military force for one bratva.

Currently, I was acting as a bodyguard for some weak pansy son of an oil oligarch who'd pissed off a Russian general by sleeping with his wife. The boy had been sent to Krasnoyarsk Prison Camp. It had taken me months to track him down since the Russians weren't exactly known for their spotless record keeping. Especially when a certain general wanted someone to disappear in the system. Now his father was using his influence and several hefty bribes to get his son out. In fact, the boy was due to leave here tonight. Technically, that made me free to take Egor up on his offer. Trouble was, I didn't like the guy, never had.

I shook my head as I tapped the ash end of my cigar onto a pile of official papers. "Get those useless sons of yours to help you." I smiled. "Oh, that's right. They got themselves shot."

A friend of mine, Mikhail Volkov, had taken them out last year for daring to kidnap the little sister of the powerful Gregor Ivanov.

I shrugged again. "Well, play a stupid game, win a stupid prize, no?"

Egor's shoulders hunched as he gripped the head of his cane more tightly. The man was broken. The only things keeping him alive among the syndicate families were his money and his connections, but they wouldn't take you far in the Russian world. Money only counted for so much if it wasn't backed by brute force and power.

Egor leaned forward, sliding a photograph across the top of the desk. "It's my daughter, Katia. She's missing."

I picked up the photo. The woman was beautiful. Her gaze seemed to pierce the camera lens. Her eyes were definitely her best feature, a stunning bright crystal blue with flecks of dark cobalt blue. They were complemented by her fair skin and glossy mink-brown hair. I frowned. "What do you mean missing?"

Egor shook his head and waved his hand in the air with frustration. "She takes after her bitch of a mother. Insisted on going off on her own to some college in Virginia. I think she found out I was planning on bringing her to Russia to marry and took off."

Katia must be the daughter from Egor's disastrous second marriage. The sons were from the first. His first wife was a sallow, beaten-down woman who died giving birth to the twins. The second had more fire in her belly, if memory served. She ran away from Egor when the daughter was still a child. It was an embarrassment for Egor as the head of the powerful Novikoff family and one of the first knocks that would lead to their current straits. Without his sons as heirs, the Novikoff legacy was in danger. It left Egor and his interests vulnerable. He must be trying to marry off his errant daughter to shore up his power.

I pocketed the photo. "So who's the lucky groom?"

"Pavel Petrov."

I grimaced. Pavel Petrov was seventy if he was a day. His sons were a nuisance to friends of mine, Vaska Lukovich and Dimitri Kosgov and their arms operations in Chicago. No wonder the chit ran away. I took out the photo and looked at it a second time. "Five million US dollars. First half wired into my usual account."

"Five million!" scoffed Egor.

The miserly bastard was worth a hundred times that amount and stood to gain tens of millions from the marriage of his family into the Petrov syndicate. I snuffed out my cigar on the wooden surface of the desk and rose. "Good luck finding her."

My hand rested on the doorknob to leave.

Egor rose as well, leaning heavily on his cane. "Wait. Fine. Five million."

I crossed to the desk and grabbed a pen. I wrote down the twenty-one-character alphanumeric code to my Swiss bank account on the edge of a piece of paper. I tore it off and handed it to him. "Half now. Half when I find her."

Egor nodded. "Agreed, but you have to bring her back to Moscow."

I gave him a curt nod and turned to leave.

Egor stopped me. "When do you start? Time and discretion are needed. The Petrovs do not know she is missing yet and I don't want them to find out."

"I'll leave tonight."

I STROLLED out of my cell around midnight. None of the cell doors were ever locked. What was the point? Escape was useless. You'd die in the frozen tundra climate only feet away from the gate. My client's son had already been picked up by his father hours earlier. My departure was a little trickier. It wasn't like the Russian prison system allowed for guests as bodyguards. I'd had to get myself thrown in here under a pretense.

Boldly walking straight up to the main gate, I stalked forward even as the nervous guard cried out a word of warning and fired several rounds into the dirt at my feet. Reaching him, I grabbed the gun and punched him in the face, knocking him out. As the alarm went out over the guard towers, I fired the semi-automatic rifle at each tower, hitting the support beams. The roofs of the two nearest towers collapsed, trapping the guards.

Tossing the rifle aside, I kicked the gate open and strolled out into the open field just as a helicopter landed.

I pulled open the side door and slid inside.

"Where to?" shouted the pilot over the din of the helicopter engine and rotor blades.

I pulled out the photo of the beautiful Katia and grinned. "America."

CHAPTER 3

uka
Worthington University, Virginia

I REACHED across the counter and grabbed the security guard by his polyester tie. I dragged him over the top of the counter until he fell in a heap at my booted feet, then leaned down and growled, "Perhaps I didn't make myself clear? I want a key to Katie Antonova's room."

The young man held up his hands, palms out. "Okay! Okay! Fuck, they don't pay me enough for this shit."

I had learned that my clever Katia had enrolled at Worthington University as a photography and business major under her mother's maiden name. She also apparently went by the more American-sounding Katie.

The man circled back around the counter and pulled out a plastic card the size of a standard credit card. He typed something on his keyboard and then shoved the card into a device. He pulled it out. "Here. She's in the Morrison Building, Room 312."

I tossed a few hundreds on the counter then took the card. As I turned to leave, he called out, "For a few hundred more, I can give you what they found."

I frowned as I turned. "What do you mean? What they found?"

The guy shrugged and motioned for me to join him behind the counter. I circled around and followed him into a cramped file room off to the right. He lifted a box off the top of a filing cabinet. The words 'Student Records 2018' had been crossed off and in a Sharpie marker was the name 'Antonova.' I reached for the box. The man swung it to the side, slightly out of my reach. "Two hundred bucks."

I smirked and reached into my pocket, pulling out the bills. I tossed them onto the floor. The man shoved the box at me as he dropped to his knees to pick up the money. I carried the box to the front room and lifted off the lid. Inside were a blue camouflage purse and a digital camera with bits of grass and mud stuck to it. Underneath those items was a pink binder.

I turned to the guard. "What is this stuff?"

He didn't look up from counting his money. "They found it outside the Arts & Culture building the day she disappeared a week ago."

I reached into her purse. Her wallet was inside with her student ID, driver's license, and money. There was also a set of car keys. A sick feeling twisted inside of my stomach. "Were the cops called?"

The guy shrugged. "Don't think so. University didn't want the bad press."

I clenched my teeth, reminding myself this man was just a flunky, otherwise I'd punch his teeth down his throat for the cavalier attitude he had about a woman disappearing off the campus.

Carrying the box through the quad, I located her dorm building. Using the key, I entered her room. From the one bed, it was obvious she didn't have a roommate I could question. I slid open the closet door. All of her clothes were on hangers in neat little rows. A roughed-up looking metallic pink suitcase rested on the floor of the closet. On her bureau were various items of makeup, a hair dryer, and a brush. The sick feeling in my stomach intensified.

This woman hadn't left.

She had been kidnapped.

Fucking Egor Novikoff.

That cheap piece of shit.

He probably hadn't even bothered to have a guard on his daughter even after her brothers were killed after that feud with the Ivanovs. Not that the Ivanovs would be responsible for this. It wasn't Gregor's style to use a woman as a pawn in a territory war. Unfortunately there were countless other syndicates including the Russians, Iranians, Italians, and a host of other nationalities that wouldn't hesitate to take advantage of an unguarded Russian mafia princess to use as leverage.

I spilled the contents of the box onto the bed. After looking through the rest of the items in her purse, I turned my attention to the digital camera. Despite the mud and slight damage to the body, the camera clicked on. I stared down at the lit LED screen as I scrolled through the images on the memory card. The first few were indistinguishable and blurry.

It was the fifth shot that captured my attention.

It was the side of a feminine face, a shoulder, and a male face behind her. He was Japanese with a long, pale face.

The next image was the man's forearm wrapped around her throat, his hand holding a cloth to her face. This time the camera lens caught Katia's eyes. The bright spark was gone from her gaze as they stretched open wide with fear. On the wrist of her attacker I could just make out a fuzzy image of something that looked like it might be a tattoo. Using the camera's controls, I highlighted the section and enhanced the pixels. A distinctive snake tattoo came into focus.

Only one syndicate used that tattoo. The yakuza. Specifically, the Inagawa-kai who were the smaller of the three main factions, but hungry for more power. I'd had run-ins with them before. All bloody and ugly.

I scrolled through the remaining images. There were several of trees, statues, a close-up of an old woman's face as she prepared lunch in probably the college cafeteria, and then Katia again. Similar to the image I still carried with me, she was staring boldly into the camera lens. This time she was holding her hair back in the wind. Her bright blue eyes were filled with intelligence and wonder.

The reality of the situation hit me like a punch to the gut.

Katia was in the hands of the yakuza and had been for at least a week.

They obviously hadn't taken her for a ransom or Egor would have been contacted, which meant they had a far darker purpose. If she was still alive, there was a very good chance she was praying for death.

I stared down at the photo and tried to imagine those gorgeous eyes sightless and blank in death.

I held the camera so tightly something cracked inside the plastic and metal body.

I inhaled deeply through my nostrils as blood coursed through my veins.

The hunt was on.

I would find Katia, dead or alive, and make the animals who took her pay.

This was no longer about the money.

This was about honor.

No one took one of our women, no matter what family she was from, and got away with it.

CHAPTER 4

*K*atie
  Chicago, Illinois

A STARTLED SCREAM woke me out of a fitful sleep. I clutched my stomach to stave off the painful cramps from lack of food.

A female voice called out from the darkness. "Hello? Is someone there?"

I was too tired and worn out to be surprised. Besides, I knew I wasn't their best leverage option. I doubted if my piece of shit father would pay a single cent for my safe return. It made sense they would grab another woman. I knew this had to be some kind of mafia territory power play with me and this other woman as the pawns.

I groaned as I tried to moisten my mouth to speak. It had been at least a few days since I last spoke to my attackers. I moved to sit up. The chain around my ankle rattled.

Finally, I rasped out, "Hello?"

"My name is Carinna. Who are you?"

Carinna? That was odd. Carinna wasn't a typical Russian name, but then again I refused to use my Russian name, Katia, so it didn't mean she wasn't connected to one of the Russian families. I opened and closed my mouth several times, trying to work my jaw and moisten my tongue before responding, "Katie. My name is Katie."

Carinna asked, "How long have you been here, Katie?"

I shifted again, my muscles crying out in pain. "What day is it?"

Carinna gestured with her head. "If that's sunlight and not streetlights, I think it might be Thursday morning."

The stupid chain rattled again as I shifted to my other hip. "They brought me here, I think, two nights ago. I've been trying to listen for the sound of the birds in the morning to keep track of the days. I don't know where here is, but they kidnapped me, I think, about a week ago, in Virginia."

Carinna answered, "We're in Chicago. Or at least I was in Chicago. I'm not sure how far we traveled after I blacked out."

Chicago? I tried to force my sleep-deprived brain to think. Who was in Chicago? It was hard to focus after several days of little sleep and even less food and water. My captors had moved me several times, always in the trunk of a car. Sometimes we drove for hours and hours at a time with no break. So far, they had refused to speak to me, but I had figured out who they were. I hadn't grown up around criminals without learning the significance of their tattoos. The men all had brightly colored tattoos of snakes around their wrists. Yakuza.

I shifted closer and reached through the darkness to place my hand on her leg. I then pressed my water bottle into her hand. "Here. Drink."

"I can't take this from you. What if—"

"I insist. Whatever their plans, they don't want us dead. They don't feed me often, but they do at least give me some food and enough water to stay alive. Drink. You'll need your strength. Are you injured?"

"I think I dislocated my shoulder. Do you know who took us?"

"The yakuza."

"The what?"

"The yakuza. They are a powerful Japanese crime syndicate."

"What would the yakuza want with me?" she asked.

"I don't know what they want with you, but I'm pretty sure I'm in this mess because of my family."

"Who is your family?"

"The Novikoffs."

"Is that Russian?"

I briefly forgot that not everyone lived in a seedy world filled with arms deals and organized crime. There were normal people who thought those things only existed on television in overblown crime dramas. I sighed. "As Russian as they come."

Carinna patted my leg. "Don't worry. My boyfriend, Maxim, will find us. He's Russian too."

I sat up. "Maxim? Maxim Konatantinovich Miloslavsky? He's in Chicago?"

If Maxim was in Chicago that meant he might be looking for me. After the first few days of being held captive, I had lost hope of my father sending help. Honestly, I had begun to think they had contacted him with a ransom demand and the cheap old bastard had refused to pay. Since I was a daughter and not a son, he had never thought I mattered much. I certainly couldn't see him paying for my safe return. He hadn't given a damn about me growing up. There was no reason to think he would start now. But knowing Maxim was in Chicago gave me hope. Maxim worked closely with the Ivanovs and also with Dimitri Kosgov and his partner, Vaska Rostov. Perhaps help was on the way. There was hope for a rescue after all.

Carinna paused before answering, "Yes. You know Maxim?"

For the first time in a week, I smiled. "Yes, I know Maxim. I was there when he got his piercing."

It was one of the few court-ordered visits I had paid to my father over the summer when I turned eighteen. I was going to piss him off by getting my nose and nipples pierced. Maxim found out and followed me to the tattoo and piercing parlor along with Damien, Gregor Ivanov's brother. When I got nervous, Maxim stepped in and offered to go first.

At Carinna's shocked gasp, I recalled Maxim's *other* piercing. "Oh, God! No! Not *that* piercing, the other ones. Although I thought *that* piercing was just a rumor."

"No, it's very real. So you and Maxim were... friends?"

I laughed. "Hell, no. He's a little too laid-back for my taste. Besides, he's Russian. I promised myself I would never date a Russian. We hung out together when he was working with the Ivanovs a few years ago. I had wanted to get my nipples pierced, but was worried it would be painful, so Maxim offered to do it first as a kind of a joke. The moment I saw that piercing gun, I practically passed out and never went through with it."

Carinna gingerly took a sip of my water. "Well, I'm sure by now he knows I'm missing. It won't be long before he finds us."

"That's what I thought a week ago. I could have sworn my father would have sent someone to find me. I even thought I overheard them talking about a man tracking them down, but I have to be honest, I was starting to lose hope."

She lifted her arm over my shoulders to comfort me. "Don't lose hope. Maxim is going to save us both. I promise. We just have to stick together and stay alive until they do. Any idea why these yakadoodles took us?"

"The yakuza, and from what I've overheard, Kiyoshi is in charge. He's here to establish a guns trade business, but first they have to get rid of the Russians who already have a lock on the market both here and on the East Coast."

"So what does kidnapping us solve?"

"Their plan is to distract the men so they are more focused on finding us than on protecting their business interests. They had planned on grabbing Samara and Yelena. They're the wives of Gregor and Damien Ivanov, but they were too well protected, so they targeted me instead. No one gave a damn about my protection, I guess. Then they came here to grab Emma. She's Dimitri's wife, but she's pregnant right now and they were worried she'd slow them down."

Carinna nodded in understanding. "So they grabbed me instead."

"Bingo."

"Well, that's where they fucked up, because we're going to get out of here."

My eyebrows rose in surprise. "We are? Look, I've tried countless times, but—"

"You were alone then. You have me now."

"You're right. We can't let the men have all the glory in rescuing us. These Russian men are far too arrogant as it is. What's your plan?"

"When they dumped me in here, did you happen to see them bring in my purse or backpack?"

I frowned and gestured across the vacant space to a lone chair several feet away. "It was pitch black, but I heard them put something over there just as they were leaving."

She pointed to the chair. "That's my purse."

I shook my head. "The first thing they would have done was look for your cell phone and tossed it out."

Carinna smiled. "Yes, but they probably missed the gun hidden in my makeup bag."

I returned her smile. I liked her already.

CHAPTER 5

Luka
Chicago, Illinois

WE WERE CLOSE. In the last few days, with the help of Maxim and Vaska, we had methodically eliminated most of the yakuza in Chicago. One by one we were taking them out. Now I was just waiting on some final intel from Vaska's sources on Kiyoshi and his right-hand man. There was a good chance he was holed up in a safehouse on the Southside. If that was true, we were going to pay him a visit tonight and hopefully, finally learn where they were keeping the girls. And the moment we did, hellfire would rain down on them. This was no longer about guns or territory. This was about honor. You didn't hurt our women and get away with it. Ever.

At least we knew they were alive. All the reports from our sources told us they were keeping the women alive as leverage.

After pacing my hotel room like a caged animal, I opened my laptop and clicked on the only folder I kept on the desktop. It was the downloaded images from another memory disk I found in Katia's purse as well as the one from the camera found in the bushes. I flipped through the images taken the moment she was kidnapped. Once again, I couldn't help but admire her fiery determination and strength of will. It took a great deal of courage to think clearly enough in the middle of getting snatched to take photos of your captor.

I flipped past the last few images to look at her work.

There was no denying she was an extremely talented photographer. These weren't photos. They were art. She seemed to favor photographs of other artists at work. There was an entire series of ballet dancers. Katia photographed the fluid beauty of their movements so perfectly they looked as if they would leap through the computer screen. There was another series of photographs taken of student painters. They were close-up photos of the artists' faces as they observed their own creations. In each photograph, Katia managed to capture an image of the painting reflected in the artist's eye. They were stunning.

I clicked through the images to get to new ones I hadn't reviewed yet. There was yet another artist series. This time they were close-ups of hands working the clay on a pottery wheel. The details in each image were visceral.

I continued to click through the images. Then stopped and stared.

It was a black-and-white image of Katia, naked from

the waist up.

It was taken in front of a bathroom mirror. The digital camera obscured half her face, but her gaze was still direct and unashamed. She stared at her own naked body with a frankness that was as startling as the nudity itself. Her full breasts hung heavy on her slight frame. Her nipples were puckered and erect. I could just imagine the cold tile floor her bare feet were probably standing on.

Her waist tucked in before her hips flared out just before the bathroom counter cut off the rest of the view.

My breath quickened as I flipped to the next photo. In this one she had turned around. Holding the camera high over her shoulder, she had taken a picture of her naked back. As if to torment the viewer, the bathroom counter cut off the view of her body at the top swell of her pert ass. Although if you looked closely, you could see two tiny dimples on either side of her spine.

My tongue flicked out over my lower lip, wanting to taste those dimples.

I flipped to the next photo.

"Fuck."

I reached for my belt buckle and unzipped my jeans as I stared at her image. It was without a doubt the most innocently erotic thing I had ever seen. Katia was stretched out on some pillows. Her long hair flowed around her head and over her shoulders to gently cover her breasts. You could see a hint of the inner curve of her left breast and nipple. Her right breast was completely exposed with a long lock of hair curling underneath the curve. Her slim arm was stretched out as if beckoning a lover.

A surge of jealous wrath ripped through my body.

The urge to find the man and rip his throat out ran strong.

I wanted to be the lover she was beckoning.

I will be the lover.

This wasn't about finding her for her father anymore.

This was about finding her for me.

I needed to know the sound of her voice. I craved to know the feel of her skin. I wanted to watch her eat and see her smile. In none of the photos I had seen so far had she been smiling. Not one. I wanted to be the man who made her smile. Over these last few days, I had gotten to know her through her photography work and had built this image up in my mind, and now I was only a few hours away from learning if it was real.

I stared at her eyes. Even though the image was black-and-white, my mind filled in the details of her bright crystal blue gaze. I wanted to see those eyes stare up at me as I thrust inside her tight body.

I pulled my cock free and fisted the length.

I stared at her mouth. Her full lips were partially open. I imagined biting the lower lip and then licking the wound with my tongue. Would she taste as sweet as she looked?

My fantasy took hold.

In a few hours, Katia would become a reality; for now I wanted the fantasy.

I stroked my cock as I imagined her standing naked before me. My large hands would span her waist as I lifted her high and threw her onto the bed. Her eyes would cloud with fear as I pressed my weight down on her, forcing her legs open. The darkness inside of me called to the fear, feasted on it. I wanted to feel her tremble under my hand. I wanted her to beg me to be gentle, only to endure the ferocity of my caress.

My tongue would lick and lave her breasts before sinking my teeth in deep, wanting to taste the salty tang of her blood on my tongue.

I stroked my cock harder as I envisioned her writhing underneath me, her small hands holding onto my shoulders as I kissed and licked her neck. I'd whisper all the dirty, nasty things I wanted to do to her innocent body into her ear as my cock sought entrance into her tight pussy.

I was a big man and she was so small. There was no way I would fit without tearing her. I thrust in deep anyway, swallowing her scream as I baptized our lovemaking with almost virginal blood. Yes, virginal. She may have had a man before me, but none my equal. With every thrust I would erase her body's memory of any other man's touch.

I stroked my cock harder as my hips lifted off the bed.

My fantasy shifted.

Now she is bent over the bed, her ass in the air. I'm standing over her with my belt in my hands. Her beautiful face is streaked with tears as she begs me not to punish her. I lift my arm and bring the belt down across both her ass cheeks. Her body rocks from the impact as her small hands fist the covers. She buries her face in the blankets as I swipe the belt across her delicate skin again and again. I revel in the deep pink flush blooming on her bottom, knowing how her hot skin will feel against my hips as I thrust in deep. I need this release as much as she does. She'll have to learn to love the kiss of a leather belt if she is to be with me. I'll teach her to love it.

My balls tightened as the pressure increased to an almost painful degree.

I let out a low growl as I stroked harder.

I imagined my hands spreading open her cheeks, baring her cute, puckered hole. In my fantasy I could feel her shame and fear, almost taste it as I ran my thumb over her dark hole, all while telling her in graphic detail how I was going to pound into her ass till she screamed for mercy. In my mind's eye, I lined my cock head up to her entrance. I had a hard grip on her hips as she struggled to crawl away from me. I pushed, watching the hole slowly open from the pressure of my cock.

Just then, I came.

I leaned over to my side, spilling my seed on the blanket as wave after pulsing wave hit me.

Jesus Christ.

Never in my life had I had such an intense experience from just jerking myself off.

Damn, this woman was the best sex I'd ever had, and I hadn't even touched her yet.

Breathing heavily, with my free hand I flipped to the next photo. It was a close-up of her lying on the bed, her eyes half closed. I stroked the screen where her cheek was. Soon, I'd have her in my arms and my fantasy would become flesh.

And if she resisted?

Well, I had plenty of intriguing ways to persuade her to submit.

CHAPTER 6

Katie

I LEANED over Carinna from behind. "Wait. Wait till he gets closer. We can't risk you missing."

Carinna held the gun in her hand. Kiyoshi and his men had just come barreling through the door. It was obvious from his appearance and agitated state that something was wrong. Hopefully it meant that Maxim, Dimitri, and Vaska were hot on his trail.

Kiyoshi came closer. They were halfway across the lengthy warehouse floor. In another few moments they would be on top of the bare mattress where Carinna and I both knelt.

"Almost there," I whispered over her shoulder. "Steady. Steady. Aim for Kiyoshi… now!"

Carinna raised her gun high and fired.

Fuck.

She missed, like really missed. The shot went wide by a mile. Passing Kiyoshi and his men, the bullet lodged in the doorjamb across the warehouse, splintering the wood just as Maxim and another beast of a man I didn't recognize came storming through.

Oh, my God. We were saved.

Despite the fight that ensued, there wasn't a doubt in my mind the Russian men would prevail over the yakuza.

As Maxim took on one of the men, the man he was with tackled the second guy, impressively knocking him unconscious with one heavy punch to the jaw.

I grabbed Carinna to get her attention and held up the gun she had dropped after firing it. "Take it. We have to try again. "

Carinna looked at me with wide eyes. "Are you crazy? I almost killed Maxim with that last shot."

I stretched out the chain that was attached to her ankle. "Not them. This. Fire at the chain."

"What if I miss?"

I looked at her calmly and shrugged. "Don't miss."

Carinna stood and pointed the gun at the floor close to the chain several feet away from her foot.

After inhaling deeply and releasing the breath slowly, she fired.

She had hit the chain! She was free. "Now run!" I yelled.

Just as she turned to do as I commanded, one of the yakuza grabbed her from behind, wrapping his forearm around her throat. Without hesitating, I grabbed the slack chain still attached to my own ankle between my fists and launched at the man. Using the chain around his neck as leverage, I leapt onto his back, squeezing his sides between my knees.

I pulled with all my might, but I was weakened after days of no sleep or food. The yakuza henchman easily flung me off his back. I sailed through the air, slamming into the wall before slowly sliding to the floor. Dazed, I shook my head as I tried to rise to my knees. Through blurry eyes, I watched Maxim charge at the yakuza who just attacked us.

The moment Carinna was set free she ran across the floor to attack Kiyoshi who was curled up on the floor after the fist pounding he received from Maxim. She kicked him in the ribs several times.

I smiled as I held up my hand to inspect the bump on my head caused by the wall when I crashed into it. I knew I liked her.

Maxim ran over to Carinna and enclosed her in his arms, holding her close. He caressed her face and kissed her mouth. I couldn't hear what they were saying but it was clear the two of them were deeply in love. My heart gave a small leap of jealousy. I had never had that. Probably never would. I wondered what it felt like to have a man be so completely devoted to you.

Carinna's body went limp. In alarm I sat up and tried again to rise to my feet. I shouldn't have worried. Maxim swept her up into his arms.

"Careful of her arm," I called out.

"What's wrong with her arm?" he asked as he inspected her for injuries.

"She dislocated her left shoulder trying to fight them off," I responded.

Maxim kissed Carinna's forehead as he whispered something to her unconscious form. My attention was diverted from them by the approach of the other man.

I didn't recognize him, although from his arrogant demeanor and visible tattoos it was obvious he was Russian. The man was huge. Like The Rock huge. The fabric of the T-shirt he had on was clinging for dear life around his enormous biceps. The shaved head and insane number of tattoos certainly didn't help in allaying my concern.

The mountain of a man approached me as he reached behind him to pull out a gun.

What the fuck?

Before I could react, he pulled the chain around my ankle taut. "Turn your head." Without even questioning the authority in his voice, I obeyed. He fired the gun into the floor, breaking my chain.

He then went down on his haunches and attempted to lift me into his arms. "My name is Luka. Your father sent me to find you, Katia."

I batted his arms away. "It's Katie and I don't need your help."

Now that I was no longer chained to the wall, I could rescue my own damn self. I certainly didn't need anyone's help who was sent by my bastard of a father. I scrambled to my knees and braced a palm against the wall as I struggled to rise. The moment I did, my knees buckled. The beast was there to catch me. Against my protests, he lifted me into his arms and made his way over to Maxim and Carinna.

Through clenched teeth, I ordered, "Put me down!"

Luka responded with a grin, "*Izvini. Ya ne govoryu po-angliyski.*"

I fumed as I crossed my arms and tried to keep my body from pressing against his. "You do too speak English, you big gorilla. *A teper' opusti menya!*" I rarely if ever spoke the Russian from my childhood, preferring American English. In fact, I barely remembered the language, but I did remember a few phrases. "Put me down now" was one of them. I had to use that a lot as a young girl being tortured and teased by my two sadistic older brothers.

His eyebrow rose. "So the little Russian princess remembers her mother tongue."

My lips thinned at being called a Russian princess. I turned my head and refused to speak to him any further, but not without first muttering under my breath in French, "*Gorille stupide.*"

He tightened his grasp on my legs and waist. "*Je parle français aussi, princesse.*"

So he was an educated beast. Great.

CHAPTER 7

Katie

My body trembled as we exited the warehouse and were met by the cold winter night air. Luka tightened his grasp on me.

He leaned down and gently kissed the top of my head. "Don't worry, princess. I'll have you at the hospital soon."

Red and blue lights illuminated the abandoned parking lot as an ambulance pulled up, sirens blaring. The paramedics opened the back doors and ran up to Maxim and Carinna first. Maxim refused to let go of Carinna. Instead, he climbed into the back of the ambulance, settling her on his lap.

Luka was carrying me in the same direction.

I turned and grasped his shirt. "No! Please, no hospitals."

He frowned. "You've been through an ordeal. You need to see a doctor."

I shook my head violently as the trembling caused my teeth to chatter. "No hospitals."

My mother, Alina, died in a hospital after a long and grueling battle with cancer. I still remember the acrid scent of bleach mixed in with her perfume as I kissed her hand one last time. I couldn't do it. No, absolutely not. No hospitals.

Luka held me tight. "All right, princess. Have it your way. No hospitals."

He motioned the paramedics away. Walking in the opposite direction of the ambulance, he carried me over to a large motorcycle.

He placed me on my feet, but kept his arm around my waist as if he was worried I'd fall. "Fuck. I only have my bike with me."

"That's okay. I'm fine. Just get me away from this place."

He reached into a saddlebag on the back of the bike and pulled out a heavy black leather jacket. As if I were a child, he lifted up one arm and put it through the sleeve, then the other. Standing in front of me, he zipped up the jacket. It was far too large and felt like I had just been wrapped in a cozy leather blanket.

Luka then straddled the bike.

I approached from the side and started to lift my leg over the back.

Before I could complete the maneuver, Luka placed his hands around my waist and lifted me off the ground as if I were nothing more than a doll. Holding me over the bike, he commanded, "Wrap your legs around my waist," as he slowly lowered me down.

I was seated facing him with my legs wrapped tightly around his body. "Shouldn't I just hold on from the back?"

His hand brushed my ass as he reached around me to turn the ignition. "No. I can't risk you losing your grip and falling off."

I huffed. "I think I'm perfectly capable of holding on while riding a motorcycle."

He stroked my cheek and smiled. "I love that you think you are, but you've been through a lot. Soon the shock is going to wear off, your adrenaline is going to plummet, and exhaustion is going to hit you like a ton of bricks. I can't risk that happening while we're riding."

It was stupid, but a small part of me was super annoyed that he was right.

Still, this was definitely awkward. It was too… intimate. I wasn't just holding on to him or sitting on his lap; I was wrapped around him like a needy clinging vine.

"Put your arms around me."

After a moment's hesitation, I placed my arms around his waist. The heat of his body permeated his thin shirt. He placed a hand on the back of my head. He pushed down till I was resting my head against his chest, snuggled within the warmth of his embrace and pressed into his body.

The bike tilted as he kicked up the kickstand. Then wobbled a little as he gave it some gas. The bike jerked into motion. Instinctively, I clutched at him tighter.

We took off through the empty parking lot. I peeked over his shoulder and watched as the dim outline of the warehouse was swallowed up in the darkness. My nightmare was over.

Soon, there would be time to wonder why my father had sent Luka. I didn't trust it was just fatherly devotion or love. But not now.

I settled deeper into Luka's embrace, holding onto him tightly as he navigated the twists and turns that would lead us to the highway and back to civilization. I wasn't sure where we were, but I could see the outline of a city skyline in the distance, so I assumed we weren't that far away from Chicago.

He didn't smell like cologne. More like clove tobacco, sweat, and leather.

In the warm strength of his arms, exhaustion took over.

I was only dimly aware of when the motorcycle stopped moving. Somehow, he managed to hold me in his arms while swinging his leg over the bike. He wrapped one arm around my back and the other under my ass and kept me close as he walked into what must have been a building. I tried but couldn't open my eyes. I was too tired. I felt the lifting motion of an elevator then heard the soft ping as the doors opened.

After a few moments, Luka laid me down on a bed. All I could feel was the soft, cloud-like down bedcover as it swallowed my body. He slipped my shoes off and covered me with another throw blanket from the sofa. Sleep overtook me.

* * *

SOMETIME LATER, I became aware of quiet voices speaking nearby. My eyes fluttered open. From what I could tell, I was in a hotel room. Still, some hospitals had fancy rooms that looked like hotel rooms.

"She's in here, Doctor."

My eyes flew open as I sat upright, fully awake now. "No, you promised!"

Luka sat on the edge of the bed. He cupped my shoulders and pushed me back down onto the bed. "I promised no hospitals. I didn't promise no doctors. Dr. Stevens is a friend of Dimitri Antonovich Kosgov. He's here to look you over."

Dr. Stevens leaned over. "Hello, Katia."

I frowned. "My name is Katie."

Dr. Stevens exchanged a look with Luka who nodded. "Call her Katie."

Dr. Stevens nodded in return as he placed his medical bag on the nightstand.

Luka stood and paced a few steps away. "She has an injury to her ankle. I'm not sure about… other injuries." His voice was tight and strained.

The doctor nodded. "We'll give her a thorough examination." He pulled the blankets off me. "Now, Katie, I need to remove your clothes so I can make sure you don't have any injuries."

Luka was by my side in an instant. "The hell you do."

The doctor straightened. "Mr. Siderov, I cannot ensure that she is not injured if we don't remove these filthy clothes and inspect her."

I started to tremble again.

Luka stared down at me, his expression thunderous. Without looking at the doctor, he said to him, "Get out."

The doctor huffed. "What?"

Luka motioned with his head. "Wait in the other room. I'll take care of it."

"But…"

Luka turned on him. "I've been in enough skirmishes and around enough military medics to know how to triage a body. Now wait in the other room."

"I hardly think that compares—"

Luka grabbed the man by the shirt collar and walked him backward. "You're not seeing my woman naked. Now get the fuck out. I will call you back in when we are ready."

With that he shoved the doctor out of the room and slammed the hotel bedroom door shut.

Luka approached and sat on the edge of the bed. He reached for the hem of my shirt.

I gripped it tightly, keeping it pulled down.

He placed his massive hand over mine. "Don't fight me on this."

I protested, "I'm not injured."

"I need to see for myself. I need to make sure they—" He swallowed and looked away briefly before continuing, "I need to make sure the bastards didn't… hurt you."

"They didn't touch me if that's what you mean. Not in that way."

The relief was evident in his gaze. "I still need to make sure you're okay."

I twisted my hands into my already ruined top. "I'm fine."

He dug his fingers into my fists, wrenching my grasp open. Before I could stop him, he had my shirt pulled over the top of my head. I crossed my arms over my chest, covering up my pink lace bra.

He reached for the button fastening to my jeans.

I tried to twist my legs to the right, but his hands held my hips down.

My eyes filled with tears as he slowly lowered the zipper.

"Lift up your hips," he commanded.

I turned my head to the side and did as I was told, knowing there was no point in fighting him. He was far too large. The top of my head barely reached his shoulder. I'd never stand a chance against his brute strength.

Luka slipped my jeans off me. I was left in only a pair of cream lace panties and my bra.

Keeping my head averted, I whispered, "There. You happy? I'm not injured."

"Not yet." He placed his warm hands around my ribcage.

I gasped at the contact of his skin on mine. "What are you doing?"

"I need to check for broken bones."

"I think I'd know if I'd broken a bone!" I protested.

He shook his head. "You'd be surprised what the body can conceal from the brain during trauma."

His hands moved over my ribcage, the sides of his thumbs caressing along each rib bone, checking for a break. I stared down at his hands. They were darkly tanned, tattooed, and slightly callused. The knuckles had white starburst scars over them. The signs of a fighter.

In the darkened warehouse and parking lot, I hadn't gotten a chance to see him clearly, but now by the soft light of the lamp in the hotel bedroom, I could finally study his features. His face was all hard angles with deep, hooded eyes, which gave him a sinister appearance. His nose was slightly crooked, a clear sign it had been broken, probably more than once. Tattoos covered his arms, hands, and neck. They were dark and faded so I couldn't quite tell what the different symbols were. His eyes were an unsettling dark gray. I'd never seen eyes like that on someone. If circumstances were different, he would make for a fascinating photography subject. The sharp planes of his face and his unusual eye color would create an intriguing photo.

His fingers trailed over my stomach.

My breath hitched.

His gaze clashed with mine. As his fingertips brushed the waistband of my panties, my eyes widened. For several heartbeats, his fingers lingered, tracing the scalloped lace edge. Was he going to pull my panties down? Would I resist if he did?

After an eternity, his hands moved. He ran his palms over my thighs, down to my calves and back again. I had to bite my lower lip to stifle a groan.

Did he know?

Could he tell that no one had ever touched me like this before?

His hands cupped my shoulders. They moved down my arms and back. This time the sides of his hands brushed the outer curves of my breasts. I inhaled sharply.

His gaze shot back to mine and held. Without taking

his eyes off mine, he shifted his hands to gently cup the undersides of my breasts through my lace bra. I licked my dry lips.

From somewhere deep inside his chest, I could have sworn I heard a growl.

After another achingly long moment, he moved his hands over my breasts and up to my neck. He speared his fingers into my hair, caressing my head. The movement pulled me up to a half-seated position. My breasts brushed his chest.

I could feel his breath against my cheek when he spoke. "I need to make sure you didn't bump your head too badly."

I almost wished I had. It would explain my insanely submissive attitude to having this Russian gorilla of a man, who I didn't even know, touch me in ways I'd never let another man.

He released my head and returned his attention to my legs. He ran his hand down my leg and bent my knee to place my foot in his lap.

He lightly brushed the ring of red skin caused by the chain. "Does it hurt?"

My mouth went dry. I couldn't speak. I knew he was talking about the cuts to my ankle, but all I could focus on was that the ball of my foot was less than an inch away from his cock. I could see it straining against his jeans. It intimidatingly ran down his thigh. If I moved my foot ever so slightly, I would be touching it.

He caught and followed my gaze. My cheeks flamed a bright red as he raised a single eyebrow and flashed me a knowing smirk.

Angry at being caught ogling his junk, I tried to pull my foot back. He wrapped his strong hand around it. No matter how hard I tried to pull back, I couldn't break his grasp. Keeping his intense gaze on mine, he deliberately pushed the bottom of my foot against his cock. He let out a low groan as he used my foot to apply pressure to his shaft. I watched, fascinated, as his hips thrust forward.

His breath was heavy as he asked, "Like what you see, princess?"

I bristled. "Stop calling me princess."

His lips twisted in a smirk. "How about I just call you mine?"

CHAPTER 8

Katie

Tugging my foot out of his grasp, I pulled on the blankets to cover my body as I slid over to the other side of the bed. "I think you're finished."

Luka winked. "Not by a long shot, princess."

He rose and opened the bedroom door and motioned for the doctor to enter.

"There are no broken bones or visible injuries except for the cut on her ankle," reported Luka.

Dr. Stevens nodded. "Let me see."

Shifting my gaze between the two of them, I held the blankets tight to my chest as I pushed my foot out from under them, only up to my calf. The doctor nodded again. He rummaged in his bag and pulled out a small white plastic jar. "Clean the cut. Then use this salve. If it starts to show signs of infection, call me. I'll write her a prescription for an antibiotic."

Before Luka could respond there was a knock on the door. Luka called out for them to enter. A hotel staff member wheeled in a cart covered in silver domes, bowed, and left without saying a word.

Dr. Stevens nodded in approval. "Good, good. Food, fluids, and rest. That is what she needs. In case she can't sleep…" He rummaged through his bag a second time and pulled out an unlabeled orange prescription bottle. He shook the bottle and several pills rattled at the bottom. "Give her one of these, but only one. Three of them would put out a horse." He placed the bottle on the nightstand.

I stared at it in horror. "What kind of doctor just has tranquilizers on him?"

Luka answered for Dr. Stevens as he pulled out a wad of cash and counted off several bills. "The discreet kind. Thank you for your time, Doctor."

Dr. Stevens grabbed the cash and left.

My eyelids drooped. I tried to stay awake, to stay alert, but exhaustion overtook me.

* * *

As I stretched under the cozy cocoon of blankets I glanced at the bedside clock and was alarmed to see that several hours had passed. It was amazing how a few hours of sleep could make you feel like a new person—or at least like someone who wasn't kidnapped and spent the last few days chained to a wall.

The sound of clothes rustling caught my attention.

Luka rose from the small sofa near the end of my bed. "What do you want to eat? I have ordered you a burger, a small pizza, a pasta dish, and some cake," he asked as he headed out of the bedroom into the main living room area.

Was he watching over me as I slept?

I propped myself up against the headboard. "I'm not hungry."

He returned to the doorway and leaned against the doorframe. "You have two options here. You select something and eat it. Or I select something and feed it to you."

I crossed my arms. "Are you this mean to your girlfriend?"

He smirked. "I'm a grown man, babygirl. I don't have girlfriends. I have women I like to fuck."

My cheeks burned at his bold answer. I didn't know why I'd fished to learn if he had a girlfriend. It wasn't like I cared. "I want to get a shower first."

He frowned. "You really should eat."

"I haven't had a shower in a week. I promise I'll eat after."

"You can have a bath."

I wrinkled my nose. "I'd rather just have a shower."

He nodded. "Very well." He strolled further into the room and lifted his T-shirt over his head, baring his heavily tattooed chest, and tossed it aside. He then reached for his belt buckle.

I sprang up to my knees, uncaring that the blanket had dropped to around my waist. "Wait! What are you doing?"

"You are weak from your time in captivity. I cannot

trust you won't fall in the shower, so I will take one with you to be safe."

I snorted. "You fucking wish. No way!"

He slipped the leather strap through the first ring of the buckle. "Make your choice, Katia. A shower with me, or a bath."

"It's Katie and I'll take the bath."

He pushed the leather strap back through the loop and turned and headed through a door that I assumed led to the bathroom.

I called after him, "You big bully!"

All I heard was his laughter, and then the roar of a tub faucet.

After several minutes he returned. "Do you want me to carry you?"

I shot out of the bed, dragging the blanket around me as I went. "Nope!" I raced past him and through the bathroom door. I slammed it shut and locked it.

Leaning against it, I let out a sigh. I hadn't had a moment to process any of this shit and didn't want to start now. I wanted to get clean and then figure out what my next move would be. I looked over at the tub and had to swallow a squeal of pleasure. He had filled it with soft, silky bubbles. Tearing off my panties and bra, I sank into the tub and leaned back with a sigh.

For the first time, I glanced around. In addition to the enormous tub there was a glass shower and lots of white and gold marble. Whatever hotel this was, it was swanky. That should definitely raise alarm bells since there was no way in hell my father was paying to put me up in this kind of luxury. Locking that thought in the *for later* box, I sank lower in the tub till the bubbles tickled my chin. Reaching for a washcloth, I added even more bath soap and scrubbed every inch of my skin till it glowed.

I closed my eyes and leaned my head back. I was finally feeling human again.

Unbidden, thoughts of Luka crept into my consciousness.

The sight of him without his shirt on. Holy hell, the man was big. Like *big*. Like muscles on top of muscles. His chest was covered in super scary-looking tattoos that only seemed to emphasize his toned abs. And then there was the feel of his cock against my foot and his hands on my body.

My palm slid along the top of my thigh. I pretended it was Luka again. Closing my eyes tight, I slipped my hand between my thighs. My fingertip slid between the folds of my pussy to find my clit. Again, I thought of Luka and the erotic, terrifying thrill I'd felt the moment he'd reached for his belt. Was he serious? Was he the type of man who would actually whip off his belt and punish a girl for being bad? I bit my lip as I pressed my fingertip to my clit. I bet he was. I bet he was the type to growl at you to get on your knees and crawl to him as he pulled out his cock.

I circled the tip of my finger around the tiny bud of nerves, alternating between soft and light pressure.

He practically screamed the dirty sex type. He probably liked to spank his women as he fucked them.

I barely stifled a groan as my back arched.

"Don't stop," growled Luka.

My eyes flew open. "Oh, my God! What are you doing in here?"

Water splashed over the edge of the tub as I scrambled to cover myself.

He placed the plate of cake he had been holding on the bathroom counter and stalked toward me. His hooded brow was low as his gray wolf eyes pierced me. "I said, don't stop."

I hunched lower in the water. Spitting out the taste of soap bubbles as I searched the bottom of the tub for the washcloth to cover my breasts. "I locked the door!"

He reached for his belt buckle. "And I unlocked it. I gave you an order."

My cheeks burned hot. How long had he been watching me? Did he know what I had been doing under the cover of the sudsy water? Of course he knew, I chastised myself.

He whipped his belt free from his jeans and kicked off his shoes. "I'm not going to tell you again, princess. Keep touching yourself."

I gathered the fading bubbles closer to cover my chest. "Get out!"

With his jeans half-undone, he sat on the edge of the tub. He reached over and grabbed my face, holding me just beneath my jaw. "Tell me you weren't just thinking about me as you played with that pretty pussy of yours," he snarled. "Tell me you weren't remembering the feel of my hands on your body."

I whimpered but couldn't respond.

He caressed my neck then moved his hand further down. He cupped my right breast and squeezed. I cried out.

"Do it now," he commanded.

My hand trembled as I moved it between my legs.

"That's it, baby. Do as I tell you."

My inner thighs clenched, locking around my wrist. This was so wrong and yet so fucking hot. I rubbed my clit, harder this time.

He massaged my breast before pinching my nipple. The shock of pain sent a lightning bolt of awareness down my spine. My hips started to move. The bathwater undulated in waves, splashing onto the floor.

"Push a finger inside. I want you to get that pussy ready for me."

My mouth opened on a groan as I pushed a finger inside of myself. Then a second one.

This was going too far. I needed to stop this. Luka thought I was someone I wasn't.

He moved his hand from my breast to between my legs. Pushing my hand aside, he replaced it with his own. His fingers were much larger and thicker than mine as they entered me.

My hips shot up. "Oh, God!"

Using his free hand, he placed two fingers against my lower lip. He forced my mouth open, then pushed his fingers inside. "Suck my fingers. Show me how you'll suck my cock."

I had no idea what I was doing. I'd never even come close to sucking a man's cock in my entire sheltered life.

Luka bared his teeth before pushing a third finger inside my mouth, pushing down on my tongue. "Suck it. Hard."

His fingers thrust in and out of my pussy as I swirled my tongue around his fingers, wetting them, drawing them deeper into my mouth. As he pushed hard on his fingers between my thighs, he pushed deeper into my mouth, gagging me. Still I sucked as my hips started to buck.

"Good girl. Come for me."

My hands grasped the edge of the tub as my torso shot up the moment wave after wave of pleasure hit my body. I crashed back down into the water as I bent my knees and grabbed his wrist, holding his hand in place as my pussy clenched down on his fingers. "Yes! Yes! Fuck! Yes!"

With what could only be described as a primal roar, Luka pulled his fingers free and lifted me out of the water. A cascade of soapy water flowed over the edge as he carried me to the shower.

CHAPTER 9

*L*uka

Setting her on her feet, with my fist I knocked the shower lever, turning the hot water on full blast.

I stood there with my jeans still on as the water flowed over both of us, washing away the suds, leaving me with an unfettered view of her every curve. God, she was beautiful. From her full breasts to her hips and sexy, dimpled ass. Her skin looked like fresh cream that I just wanted to lick. I had yet to even kiss her.

Leaning her back against the tiles, I wrapped my hands around her jaw and tilted her head back. I pressed my mouth to hers, breathing her air before slipping my tongue inside. The moment the tip of her tongue touched mine, I deepened the kiss. Pressing my hips into hers, I pushed my fingers into her hair and held her face firmly as I plundered her mouth over and over again. I couldn't get enough of her taste or the feel of her tongue dueling with mine.

I reached between our bodies to cup her breast. Breaking our kiss, I leaned down to suck one nipple into my mouth. Using my teeth, I teased the sensitive flesh, loving how her back arched each time I gently bit down. I returned to her mouth.

"Open for me," I rasped against her already swollen lips. I traced her upper lip with my tongue before scraping the edges of my teeth along her full bottom lip. I had to resist the urge to bite down, wanting to taste her blood like I had in my fantasies.

I was a man possessed. All reason and civility had left my body. All that was left was a feral animal need to make this woman mine. I didn't just want to fuck her. I wanted to breed her. I wanted my seed deep in her belly, binding her to me in blood for all eternity.

I spun her around until she was facing the tiles. Lifting her arms up, I interlaced my fingers with hers and leaned in to whisper in her ear, "I'm going to fuck you so hard, you'll taste my cock in the back of your throat."

I then slapped her wet ass.

Katia let out a yelp as she tried to break my embrace.

I spanked her again, pleased when I saw my raw, red handprint appear on her pale cheek.

"Spread your legs," I ordered, spanking her again when she didn't immediately obey me.

"Wait! We can't."

I fisted her wet hair and pulled her head back. "The fuck we can't."

"You don't understand."

I tore at the fastening to my jeans, lowering the zipper the rest of the way down. Knowing I would never get the wet denim off, I jerked open the flaps and just pulled out my cock. "I understand all I need to. Your sweet pussy is going to get fucked raw."

I kicked at her feet, widening her stance even further. Reaching between her legs, I teased her pussy, feeling the silky touch of her arousal, knowing she was ready for me.

I placed my hands on her waist and tilted her hips back until she was bent almost in half. Her brown hair clung to her shoulders. I ran my hand down her back, circling each dimple above her ass cheeks with my fingertip. I spanked her ass several more times, relishing how her flesh bounced with each hit then bloomed into a fiery pink.

"Ow, that hurts!"

"It's supposed to hurt. Only through pain do we know pleasure."

I fisted my cock and bent my knees slightly, lining my hips up with hers. I placed the head of my cock at her entrance and then gripped her hips. I breathed heavily through my nose several times, trying to slow the rapid beat of my heart, knowing if I fucked her right at this moment, I might tear her in two. I tilted my head back, letting the water hit me in the face and cascade down over my shoulders and chest. My cock swelled to painful proportions. I could not hold back the tide any longer.

Pressing my fingertips into her pale flesh, I thrust forward.

Fuck. She was so goddamn tight. I barely got my cock in halfway before feeling her body clench and resist.

Katia screamed as she rocked forward. Her body flattened against the tiles. The upward motion of her torso pushed her hips forward, further burying my cock deep inside of her.

Bending my hips, I thrust again. This time with even more force, burying myself to the base in her tight heat.

Katia cried out again as she clawed at the wet tiles.

It all crashed down on me at once.

Her reaction.

The slight resistance I'd felt the moment I breached her entrance.

I leaned back and looked down between us.

Pale pink water was running down her inner thigh.

Jesus Christ.

Katia trembled against the tiles.

She was a virgin.

At least, she had been a virgin.

And I had taken her like a fucking animal.

I knew she was at least twenty-two. How had a girl in her twenties, and as beautiful as she, remained a virgin for so long?

It didn't matter.

She was mine now.

Truly and completely.

Once again, I looked down at our joined bodies and never wanted to pull my cock out.

I leaned in closer, wrapping my arms around her.

Katia resisted, trying to twist out of my embrace. "I don't want to do this anymore."

It was too late for regrets.

And far too late to stop.

I reached around her hip and teased her pussy. Pressing my fingertips between the folds to flick her clit, bringing her back to ecstasy. As I moved my fingers, I kissed her neck, whispering soothing nonsense in her ear. I rocked our bodies together, letting her get used to the feel of my cock deep inside of her. I caressed her stomach and breasts as the hot water eased her tension. When I pinched her nipple, she moaned and leaned her head back on my shoulder as her small hand wrapped around my wrist, holding my hand against her breast.

My cock swelled.

"Detka, ya bol'she ne mogu sderzhivat'sya."

Katia moaned.

Realizing I spoke in Russian and not knowing how much of the language she remembered from her childhood, I said, "Do you understand me, baby? I need to fuck you. Now."

I flattened my hand over her belly and pushed her hips back as I pulled my cock out a few inches and thrust back in to emphasize my words.

"Yes," she groaned.

"Ya ne mogu byt' nezhnym." Then I repeated, "I can't be gentle."

Before she could respond, I dragged us both out of the shower. I bent her wet body over the bathroom counter. Twisting my hand into her hair, I pulled, forcing her head back and our eyes to meet in the mirror.

Her blue gaze widened as she took in the sight of my massive body looming over her much smaller one.

I pulled back and thrust in deep.

Her mouth opened on a silent scream.

I thrust in again and again.

Her breasts were smashed against the cold marble as her body rocked back and forth with the violence of my movements.

I raised my arm, wanting to see her face the moment I spanked her ass. Her gaze followed my hand. Her lower lip trembled as her eyes glazed over. I brought my hand down on her vulnerable flesh, watching as her swollen, deep red lips opened on a cry. I then tightened my grasp on her hair as I pounded into her, feeling the pressure build deep within my balls.

"Who's fucking you, baby?"

"Oh, God, you are."

"Who owns you now?"

She didn't respond as her hand moved between her thighs. I could feel the tips of her fingers brush the base of my cock as she rubbed her clit, cresting her own orgasm.

I spanked her ass as I held her gaze in the mirror. "Answer me. Who owns you now, princess?"

A spark of the defiance I saw earlier lit within her gaze, turning her eyes from bright crystal to a blue flame. "No one owns me."

I smiled.

She'd pay for that later.

Showing her no mercy, I pounded into her until her pussy clenched around my shaft as she came a second time that night. The moment she did, I spilled my seed deep within her body.

Branding her as mine, whether she liked it or not.

CHAPTER 10

Katie

By the time Luka pulled out, my skin had started to chill. Getting no resistance from me, he lifted me into his arms and carried me back to the shower. Since it was one of those swanky luxury ones, it had a small marble bench in the corner. He sat down and held me on his lap. He then reached for the shampoo. Without saying a word, he lathered my hair. I closed my eyes and focused on the feel of his strong hands massaging my scalp.

At this moment, I only wanted to feel, not think.

Luka leaned in and rasped, "Close your eyes, baby." He placed his hand over my eyes to shield them as he tilted my head back under the shower stream, rinsing my hair clean. He then poured some conditioner into his hand and worked it into my hair. All the while, I sat there complacently on his lap.

Life had a strange way of letting you know you weren't the one in charge.

Throughout high school, there had been several boys I knew had a crush on me, that I wouldn't let get past first base. Then in college, I was more focused on my studies, which left little opportunity to even try to pursue a relationship. Somehow, my virginity went from something I was embarrassed to still have at the end of high school, to something I didn't have time to think about in college.

And then Luka came along.

I'd known the man for less than a few hours and I let him fuck me sideways, in a shower no less.

I always thought I'd lose my virginity to some fumbling boy in the back of a car or maybe to a slightly drunk frat boy in a dorm room. In any scenario it was going to be awkward and unsatisfying, with a boy who only thought he knew what he was doing. Never in my wildest imagination did I think I'd lose it to some massive two-hundred-and-forty-pound, six-foot-five Russian gorilla who played my body like a freaking violin. Especially since I'd sworn never to date a Russian.

Luka ran a soapy washcloth over my back in soothing circles before running it down my arms and legs. He then soaked the washcloth in hot water before pressing it between my thighs and holding it there.

He pushed my hair back behind my ear. "I'm sorry."

I refused to meet his gaze. "For what?"

He sighed as he continued to stroke my hair. "I should have been more... gentle."

I turned my head to look at him. Curiosity got the

better of me. "Would you have still done it if you'd known I was a virgin?"

His gaze swept over my face to stop at my mouth. He brushed his thumb over my lower lip. "Yes."

I wasn't sure what I was expecting, but raw honesty definitely wasn't it.

I climbed off his lap and moved fully under the water stream. Crossing my arms over my chest, I gave him a nervous laugh. "Not one to mince words, are you?"

Luka stood, his height dwarfing me. He reached out an arm but stopped a few inches short of touching me. "Katia…"

I swallowed. "It's Katie."

I left the shower stall. I wrapped a towel around my body and snatched up the plate of cake before leaving the bathroom.

After drying off, I looked down at my dirty T-shirt and jeans and shuddered. Casting a glance at the closed bathroom door, I listened for a moment. The shower was still running. Luka was still in there.

I crept across the suite to the black leather motorcycle saddlebags that were resting on the sofa. Flipping up the flap on the first one, I found a folded-up white T-shirt and pulled it over my head. It was so large it reached past my knees. In the second bag, I saw a familiar sight. Casting a glance over my shoulder to make sure Luka was still in the bathroom, I pulled out my blue camouflage purse. Searching the bag further, I found my digital camera. I searched the rest of the contents of his saddlebags; there was a thick roll of cash and a folded-up piece of paper. Again casting a nervous glance over my shoulder, I unfolded the paper. It was a printout of an airline reservation. Two economy class tickets to Moscow in our names, leaving in three days from Chicago.

I heard the shower tap shut off.

I quickly refolded the piece of paper and shoved it and my purse and camera back into the saddlebag I'd taken them from. As much as I hated to do so, I pulled off the T-shirt and replaced it in the other bag as well. I didn't want Luka to know I had gone snooping and found the tickets. I ran naked back to the bedroom and climbed into the center of the bed. I picked up the plate and started to eat the chocolate cake.

I was innocently sitting there in the bed with the sheet wrapped around my torso when he emerged. "You should eat something more substantial than cake."

I looked up and my mouth fell open. He was standing there with only a small white hotel towel wrapped around his hips, his thickly muscled thighs, chest, and biceps on full display. His tanned, inked skin was still wet from the shower we'd shared.

I started to speak, but only a tiny squeak came out. I cleared my throat and tried again as I focused my attention back on my dessert plate. "I kind of wanted to get dressed, but I have nothing to wear."

He rubbed his forehead. "Of course. I should have thought of that. It's a little late for any stores to be open. I'll get a personal shopper here first thing tomorrow with some clothes. Until then, you can wear one of my T-shirts." He crossed into the living room portion of the suite and returned with the same white T-shirt.

I took it from his hand and pulled it over my head again. "Thank you."

He talked to me from the living room over the rustle of clothing. "The food is probably cold by now. Did you want me to order more?"

"No, thanks."

There was the clinking sound of ice hitting glass. Luka strolled into the bedroom. He had on a pair of gray sweatpants and nothing else. He was carrying an old-fashioned glass filled with an amber liquid.

"Can I have a sip?"

He held it out to me and then pulled his hand back at the last minute. "Wait, are you even old enough to drink?" he teased.

I bristled. "I'll be twenty-two in two months; besides, I think I've earned a drink after all I've been through this week."

He nodded and handed it to me. "Just a tiny sip."

I took the glass and tilted it back. Before I could get more than a gulp, his large hand wrapped around the glass and pulled it away. "That's enough, little one. You're probably not used to whiskey and on an empty stomach it will be worse."

The fiery liquid burned a path down my throat to settle in a warm ball of fire inside my stomach.

He sat in one of the upholstered chairs in the lounge set up across from the bed and stared at me. He sat in that chair like an arrogant, self-assured man would, leaning back with his knees spread.

I pushed an icing pink rose across the plate. "So what happens now?"

Luka leaned forward and rubbed the back of his neck. "Now? Now we eat and get some sleep. Tomorrow, I'll get you some clothes."

"Are you going to escort me back to my college?"

Luka drained his glass and set it on the glass coffee table in front of him. "Let's not talk about that right now."

"I'm not going back to Russia."

"Your father wants to see you."

"I don't care. That man hasn't been in my life for years."

His eyes narrowed. "Is that why you go by Katie and use your mother's maiden name?"

I put the plate on the nightstand. "I never asked to be a Novikoff."

"Nevertheless, you are one. And the only daughter. With that comes risks, as you now know."

I pushed my chin out as I defiantly met his gaze. "I can take care of myself."

He smirked. "All evidence to the contrary."

I sprang up to my knees and crawled to the edge of the bed. "Fuck you. I'll have you know Carinna and I were in the middle of saving ourselves when you and Maxim burst in. Another few minutes and we would have met you two in the parking lot."

Luka rose and stalked toward me.

Before I could turn away, he grabbed me by the chin and tilted my head back. "Watch that mouth of yours, babygirl. And the next time you get down on your knees and crawl to me, you better be prepared to handle the consequences."

I clenched my jaw as I tore my head to the side. "Tonight was a mistake."

He grabbed my hair and held my head forward as he crouched down on his haunches. He was so tall his eyes were level with mine. "Tonight was fate, not a mistake. You can spin it however you want in that pretty little head of yours, but it happened. And it's going to happen again."

"When hell freezes over," I ground out.

He gave me a hard kiss on the lips. "Then bundle up, babygirl, because it's about to get real cold."

He rose and crossed back to the bar in the living room area and poured himself another drink. When he returned he brought the pizza back with him. He placed the plate on the edge of the bed, grabbed a slice, and then took his seat again.

My stomach growled.

Luka looked at me with an eyebrow raised. "If you think to deny yourself to spite me, it's a game you won't win, princess. Eat a fucking slice of pizza."

With a huff, I reached for a piece and took a bite. Even cold, it was heavenly. Still, I didn't want to give him the satisfaction. "Fine, I'm eating. You can leave now."

Exhaustion was starting to take hold. After this slice of pizza, all I wanted to do was curl up under the covers and sleep for days.

He cocked his head and looked at me. "I'm not going anywhere."

I stared back at him, my brow furrowed. "Does this suite have a second bedroom I'm not seeing?"

He grinned. "Nope."

My eyes widened as I shrank back until my body hit

the headboard. "You can't mean… you can't possibly think…"

"I can mean, and I do think."

"I'm not sharing a bed with you."

"You don't have a choice."

I gestured wildly toward the living room. "You can sleep on the sofa."

"No."

"Fine." I gathered the sheet from the bed around me. "I'll sleep on the sofa."

I swung my legs off the bed and had only taken two steps when Luka wrapped his arm around my waist from behind. He nipped at my ear before growling, "I'm trying really fucking hard not to throw you on that bed, spread your legs, and plow into your sweet untried body until you beg for mercy, because I know you've been through a lot and need time to recover. But if you keep trying my patience, I'm going to forget about playing the gentleman and fuck you so hard you won't be able to walk for a week. Do you understand me?"

I swallowed; unable to speak, I could only nod.

"Good girl. Now get your ass back in that bed and eat another slice of pizza. You need more food in you if you're going to get your strength back."

I scrambled to obey. Sitting in the center of the bed, I wolfed down another slice of pizza, then laid back.

Luka walked into the bathroom and returned with the blanket I had taken in there. He spread it over me and tucked the sides in over my hips as if I were a child. Just then there was a knock on the outer door. He strode to the bedroom door. "Keep quiet," he ordered before closing it behind him.

I hopped up and slowly turned the doorknob.

Luka was standing there with another man I didn't recognize. They both had their backs to me. It was only when Luka shook his hand and greeted him that I realized it was the infamous Dimitri Kosgov. I hadn't seen him since I was a pre-teen.

When Dimitri spoke his tone was soft and low. "How is she? Does she need anything?"

Luka's back straightened as he threw his shoulders back. "If she does, I'll provide it."

Dimitri handed him a small pink gym bag. "Emma packed this with some clothes. She thought Katia might appreciate something clean to wear."

Luka tossed the bag on the bar. "Thank her for us."

Dimitri waved him off. "She's used to it." He then said, "The Petrov brothers paid me a visit. Their father found out Katia was missing. They now know we got her back. Her father is demanding you put her on the next plane to Moscow. He's changing the tickets he sent you as we speak."

Luka rubbed the back of his neck. "Is he still planning to force her to marry Pavel Petrov?"

Pavel Petrov? The man was a thousand years old!

I knew my father didn't love me, but how could he think to condemn me with an arranged marriage like that?

Dimitri shook his head. Disgust was evident in his voice. "The moment her feet hit the tarmac."

Having heard all I needed to, I carefully closed the

door. I had to think fast. Scanning the room for a weapon, my eyes fell on the small pill bottle Dr. Stevens had left on the nightstand. Snatching it up, I unscrewed the cap. I poured out three pills and pressed down on them with the bottom of the pill bottle, crushing them. Scooping the dust into my palm, I crossed the room to Luka's drink. Using my finger, I scraped the tranquilizer pill dust into his drink and mixed it with my finger.

CHAPTER 11

Luka

I CAST a glance over at the closed bedroom door. I paused a moment, listening for any sounds of movement. Just in case, when I turned back to Dimitri, I lowered my voice. "Yeah, well, plans have changed."

Dimitri leaned against the door. "She's his daughter. The man has a right to dictate her future."

"He forfeited that right when he failed to protect her. He fucking knew she'd become a target for his enemies, and he left her vulnerable."

"You keep her from her family, it could start a war."

My eyes narrowed. "You threatening me, my friend?"

Dimitri held up his hands. "Absolutely not. I am now the father of a baby girl, Elizabeth. I would burn the entire world to the ground if someone tried to keep her from me."

"Yes, but you'd never abandon her to the wolves."

He nodded. "Very true." He slapped me on the shoulder. "If it is a war they want, then it is a war they will get. You will have my and Vaska's support, of course. And you know the Ivanovs will be by your side. Gregor and Damien have had a hell of a time keeping Mikhail from killing the old bastard for his part in kidnapping Nadia last year."

"Good to know."

"So what do you plan to do with her?"

I shook my head. "Not sure yet. I might stash her someplace remote until the drama blows over."

"Or Pavel dies. The man has one foot in the grave, it could happen any day now."

We shared a mirthless laugh.

Dimitri sobered and stared at me. "Luka, are you sure about this? You could be stirring up a fuckton of trouble to protect a woman you barely even know."

I stared back at him. He was right. A few months ago if someone had told me I would be prepared to put my life on the line and my reputation at risk for a spoiled little mafia princess, I would have laughed in their face. "How long did it take for you to know with Emma?"

Dimitri smiled. Even a hardened bastard like me could see the love and devotion in his eyes. "Seconds."

"Then you have your answer, my friend."

He nodded and turned to leave. "I'll come by with Vaska tomorrow. Together we will plan our attack."

I closed the door and slipped the chain back on.

I walked back into the bedroom and caught Katia standing by the window holding my glass of whiskey. The sheet draped around her might as well have been a ball gown. She looked stunningly beautiful without makeup and even with the slight shadows under her eyes.

She blushed. "I was just stealing another tiny sip."

I crossed to her and slipped an arm around her waist. Taking the glass from her fingers, I drained the contents and set it on the glass coffee table. "Come, let's get you back in bed."

She was surprisingly submissive as I placed a hand at her lower back and led her to the bed. She lay down and allowed me to cover her with a blanket. I pivoted and crossed the room to turn off the lamp near the lounge area.

As I took a few steps, my head swam. I raised a hand to my forehead. The entire room wobbled and became unfocused.

Alarmed, I turned and stared at Katia. "What did you do?"

Her eyes narrowed as she rose from the bed. "What I had to."

I lunged for her, but my body was already succumbing to the drug.

I stumbled and crashed through the glass coffee table.

Then everything went black.

CHAPTER 12

Katie

"Holy fuck!"

I ran over to Luka. Grabbing a pillow from a nearby chair, I swept the shards of glass aside and gingerly stepped close to him.

Fuck!

I killed him.

Holding my breath, I leaned down and placed two fingers at his throat, feeling for a pulse. I let out a sigh of relief when I felt his heartbeat through my fingertips. Okay, not dead.

Setting the pillow on the floor, I kneeled on it and placed my hands on his shoulder and side. I shoved with all my might. He barely budged. Jesus, it was like rolling a massive tree. Finally, after two more attempts, he rolled onto his back. With the exception of a few cuts along his face and arms he seemed unharmed.

Unharmed at least with the exception of the horse dose of tranquilizers I had just given him.

I bit my lip. His face looked relaxed, almost peaceful. I knew it would not stay that way. The moment he awoke he would be like a raging bull. It was best if I was far, far away when that happened.

Racing into the living room, I spied the pink gym bag on the bar. I unzipped it and gave a cry of delight at the jeans, sweater, jacket, and pair of Converse sneakers inside. Everything fit with the exception of the sneakers being a little snug. I then raced over to his saddlebags. I flipped open the bag holding my purse and camera, grabbing them as well as the wad of cash.

I looked into the bedroom one last time.

Biting my lip, I tried to tamp down the wave of guilt that was crashing over me.

With a frustrated huff, I set aside my purse and camera and charged into the bedroom. Leaning down, I raised his head and put the pillow under it. I then used a second pillow to brush away as much of the glass as possible. Finally, I covered him with a blanket.

I then left without a backward glance.

CHAPTER 13

Luka

"Wake up, Sleeping Beauty."

Someone kicked my side. I frowned as I tried to open my eyes, but immediately shut them against the glaring light of the sun.

"Wake up, sleepyhead!"

The same person kicked me again.

With a growl, I shoved at the foot and rolled over onto my knees. I then forced down the bile rising in the back of my throat to rise to my feet. "What the fuck happened?"

Vaska chuckled as he placed his feet up on what remained of the frame of the shattered coffee table. "Well, as far as we can tell, the damsel in distress drugged Prince Charming and made a rather hasty exit out of her fairy-tale ending."

I stumbled to the bathroom as I tossed a "Fuck you" over my shoulder.

Leaning over the sink, I splashed cold water on my face.

Memories of last night flashed across my mind as I stared into the mirror. Her bent over the counter. Me deep inside of her. The look on her face the moment she came.

I returned to the bedroom. Vaska and Dimitri were now standing there with grins on their faces. "What the fuck you are two so happy about?"

Dimitri laughed. "You got the shit kicked out of you by a girl."

Vaska slapped him on the back. "To be fair, the glass table did most of the work."

"You both are assholes." I moved into the living room area and grabbed my saddlebags for a change of clothes. They followed me.

Dimitri sipped his coffee and said, "If you are looking for your cash, she took it all."

I opened the bag and looked inside. Her purse, camera, and the cash were gone. It actually made me feel better. At least the minx had some money on her and it was only about fifteen thousand, pocket change.

I pulled out a pair of jeans and a black T-shirt. "What time is it? Have you put eyes on the airport and train terminals?"

Dimitri moved out of my way as I stormed past him to the bathroom. He called through the door, "Don't worry, my friend. We are on it. She hopped on a red-eye to Arlington, Virginia late last night. We gave Gregor a heads-up and he put a tail on her the moment she landed. At this moment she is safely tucked away in her dorm room."

Vaska chimed in, "Sleeping like a baby. *Like you were a moment ago.*"

I opened the door as I pulled the hem of the T-shirt down over my stomach. "Have I mentioned you're an asshole?"

"Relax, this is good news!"

I snatched the coffee from his hand and took a large gulp of the piping hot liquid. "How is this good news?"

"It means she likes you."

"She drugged me. Stole from me and took off in the middle of the night to get as far away from me as possible."

Vaska beamed as he also slapped me on the back. "Exactly! When they run, it means they like you. Just ask Dimitri."

Dimitri scowled. "Keep me out of this. Right now we have to figure out what we're going to tell Novikoff and Petrov."

I grabbed my saddlebags and headed for the door. "Tell them they can both fuck off. She's mine now."

CHAPTER 14

Katie

"It must have been terrifying!"

I stared out the classroom windows, unhearing.

A hand waved in front of my face. "Hello, Earth to Katie!"

With a start, I turned my head and looked at my friend, Brooklyn. "I'm sorry, what?"

She gave me a dramatic sigh as she rolled her eyes. Her thick fake eyelashes caught in her purple bangs. She brushed them aside. "I said... it must have been terrifying. I can't imagine what it would feel like not knowing your own name!"

My chest tightened with guilt.

Brooklyn was my best friend. She was the quintessential, but also stereotypical, art student. This week her hair was purple. Two weeks ago it was bright green.

She had both a lip and a nose piercing and was fond of telling people she met that her parents named her after the place she was conceived.

I adored her.

And I also just lied straight to her face. "Yes, thank God my memory came back so quickly," I responded weakly.

I shared everything with Brooklyn except for my real name. She had no idea I was considered a Russian mafia princess, the only daughter of the powerful Novikoff family. Brooklyn would probably find it all dramatic and exciting if she did know, which could never happen.

I had to come up with some kind of cover story as to why I disappeared and heartlessly made her worry without reaching out. Since obviously I couldn't tell her the truth—that a powerful Asian crime syndicate named the yakuza kidnapped me as leverage over my equally powerful and equally criminal Russian mafia family. Duh.

So I came up with the lame excuse that after leaving the Arts & Culture building a week ago, someone on a bike knocked me to the ground. I told her I bumped my head and didn't know who or where I was. In the fall I dropped my purse and camera in the bushes, so I had no identification on me. A good Samaritan picked me up and took me to the hospital where I languished as a Jane Doe until *poof*, my memory came back late last night.

It was a stupid story but filled with just the kind of romantic dramatic details that Brooklyn would eat up.

We met when we were freshmen and for the last four years had been inseparable. Her preferred medium was sculpture and pottery, so we often spent hours together in the basement of the Arts & Culture building working on school projects. When we graduated, we even had plans to open a little gallery together. She could sell her artwork and I could display my photographs and run my photography business out of the back office.

I wasn't stupid. I knew I wouldn't be able to make a living right out of the gate just selling my prints. That was why I was also taking some rather boring business classes while still in school. I planned on being a wedding photographer until things kicked off. Some *serious* photographers would say that was selling out, but I disagreed. Besides, I loved shooting weddings, all the pageantry and dancing and laughter.

It was fun, especially since I had no plans of ever getting married myself. I saw what marriage to my father did to my sweet mother. To this day, I was convinced the cancer that took her was more a cancer of the mind and spirit. Even after she left him, my father did everything he could to make her life a living hell, all because his pride was bruised. Never would I allow myself to be leg shackled to a man like that.

It was one of the reasons why I had always refused to even consider dating a Russian man. They were too arrogant and controlling. Marriage to a Russian man would be a nightmare. Especially since, no matter how I tried to hide it, my true name and identity as a Novikoff would eventually be revealed. I'd never know if the man was in love with me, or the power my family name held among the Russian syndicates.

Hopefully, Luka would just report back to my father that I had been rescued and that I had returned to school and that would be the end of it. He would have to know by now he wouldn't be able to force me into a marriage I didn't want. I was sure my father only said he wanted me to return to Russia, like he did a few years ago, to save face. He'd want to appear to be the doting, concerned father to others in the syndicate. Family loyalty meant a great deal to Russians. It was why my mother was forced to take me for those horrific visits with my father and brothers throughout my childhood.

I rubbed my upper forearm. I swore I could still feel the bruises they gave me. Always on my arms, back, and legs, never anything in view above my clothes. It was why I favored long-sleeved shirts. No one knew about the abuse, especially my mother. If she had known, she'd have done something drastic to save me. I couldn't allow that. Even as a child, I knew the evil my father and half-brothers were capable of. I may be going to hell for it, but I was glad to hear that someone had killed my half-brothers last year. The world was better off without them. And it would be even better when my father finally died. At least he was in Russia, and up until recently, had left me alone.

Luka had reassured me that the yakuza had been taken care of and I didn't have to worry about any more attempts on my life. I really hoped that was true. All I wanted was to lead a normal, quiet life as a photographer. My brush with my family's criminal connections had only reinforced my commitment to have nothing to do with them, their world, or their money. I'd scrape by on ramen noodles and protein bars before accepting a penny from any of them.

Thoughts of Luka invaded my mind.

Was he okay?

I was sure someone, probably the hotel housekeeper, had found him by now.

He was probably furious with me, and for good reason. The man had rescued me from a terrible fate, and I repaid him by drugging him and stealing his cash.

Well, that wasn't entirely true.

He did get my virginity as payment.

My cheeks heated as I thought back to the other night. It already felt like a lifetime ago. The hot, fevered way he'd fallen on me like a ravenous wolf. It was both terrifying and exciting to be the focus of such intense, passionate energy.

It was as if I had been swept out into the middle of the ocean during a fierce thunderstorm. Every touch of his hand sent me tumbling under the dark waters as lightning struck the waves. His whispered sexual threats were like the howling winds churning the waters. Even as I tried to sort out my feelings hours later, they were still just a jumble of emotions. Fear, pleasure, excitement, pain, anticipation, trepidation.

Later, as I tried to sleep on the plane, I couldn't help wondering what it would have felt like to be cocooned within his arms. If I hadn't left, I probably would have been curled up with him at that moment, sharing his warmth. I bet it would have felt safe.

I shook my head.

There was no point in thinking about Luka.

He was a non-starter for me.

A Russian criminal with ties to my family. Nope, nope, and nope.

Professor Beramend addressed the class. "Open your textbooks to chapter fourteen, Artistic Innovations in Fifteenth Century Northern Europe."

Brooklyn groaned. "Dammit, I hate Jan van Eyck's work. This is going to be torture."

I gave her a sympathetic smile as I opened my *Janson's History of Art* textbook and flipped to the correct page.

While my professor droned on, I once again turned to stare out the window.

The roar of a motorcycle engine caught my attention. I searched the area within view but could only see the upper corner of the nearest parking lot.

My heart raced.

Stop it.

This was silly.

So what? I'd heard a motorcycle. There were probably lots of students who rode motorcycles around campus.

It didn't mean it was *him*.

Luka was probably halfway back to Russia by now.

In fact, he was probably happy to get rid of me so easily. No next morning awkward speech to pacify the silly twenty-one-year-old virgin.

Brooklyn nudged me and nodded toward Professor Beramend. I forced Luka from my thoughts and tried to concentrate on class.

Throughout the day, I swore I kept hearing that damn motorcycle. I heard it as I walked through the quad, when I exited the cafeteria, and when I was in my Business Marketing 204 class. It was like it was following me around campus. Each time, my mind spun out with all kinds of revenge fantasies. Was Luka here to kill me for taking his money? Was he going to kidnap me and toss me in the cargo hold of some plane bound for Russia?

Those were the easy ones to handle.

The difficult fantasies were the sexual ones.

I kept having the recurring fantasy that he would appear, toss me over his shoulder, then tie me to his bed and fuck me senseless for hours as *punishment* for drugging and ditching him. My cheeks heated at the thought of it. It was impossible to focus on any of my class lectures. Why the hell did I find that fantasy so arousing? It was so twisted and wrong. And yet the vision of Luka standing over me with his belt in his hand had me squirming in my seat.

I was beyond relieved when my last class of the day let out. I had a mountain of classwork to catch up on after being gone for a week. I was going to grab a sandwich and some chips from the deli on campus and head back to my room. I would bury my head in my books for the rest of the night. That's what I needed to get Luka off my mind.

As I exited the deli, the scent of clove cigarettes lingered in the air.

I pulled my hoodie up over my head and lowered my gaze as I practically ran across campus to the safety of my dorm room.

It was absolutely the fault of my over-heightened imagination that I thought I heard a sinister chuckle on the winter wind as I ran.

CHAPTER 15

Luka

SHE DIDN'T LOOK peaceful as she slept. The thin blanket and sheets were tangled about her legs as she tossed and turned. She was only wearing a silk button-up pajama top with a tiny pair of silk pajama shorts so her long slim legs were on full display. Her arm thrashed to the side and her lips parted to murmur something unintelligible in her sleep.

What disturbed her dreams?

Was it the recent trauma of the kidnapping?

Was it her father?

Or was it me?

The idea that I could be the monster stalking her dreams upset me more than I cared to admit. Especially since I was standing here watching her, wanting to be the man who slayed those monsters. I wanted to hold her body tight and kiss her furrowed brow.

Too often I was the demon. I was the man the different family syndicates called on to complete the darkest of tasks. The type of assignments a man of moral consciousness would cringe in horror at doing. I was tired of being that man. Tired of being the villain. Just once, I wanted to play the hero. I wanted to know what it felt like to be loved instead of feared. I had no family to speak of and even my friends kept me at a distance, afraid of what I was capable of. I wanted to know what it felt like to have someone look at me with love, not terror. Instead of always protecting the interests of other families, I wanted a family of my own. I wanted a son I could pass my name on to.

I looked down at Katia as she turned on her side. The pajama shorts had ridden up, exposing the cute under curve of her ass. The top had inched up as well, giving me just a glimpse of the pale skin of her abdomen.

Was she pregnant with my child already? It was improbable but not impossible.

Katia Novikova was the perfect woman for me, and it wasn't just her Russian heritage. Any woman who could come out of the trauma of being kidnapped by the yakuza for a solid week still swinging was one worth holding on to. She was smart and talented, with a fighting spirit. The kind of woman a man would be proud to have at his side. The kind of woman to bear a man strong sons.

Of course, there were obstacles.

Her father being determined to marry her into another powerful family was one. I was certain he wouldn't take kindly to his daughter being married to a mafia mercenary with no family connections.

There was also the issue of her hating my guts enough to try to kill me before running off, but that was nothing a little discipline couldn't solve.

I reached over and clicked on the small pink-shaded lamp on her bureau. It cast a soft rose glow throughout the small dorm room.

Katia stirred in her bed before opening her eyes.

She started and shrank back against the metal rail headboard. "How did you get in here? The door was locked."

I smirked. "I unlocked it."

She raised her arm and pointed. "If you want your money, it's in the top drawer of my bureau. I only used about seven hundred for an airline ticket and cab ride. I'll pay you back."

I reached for my belt buckle. "Oh, princess, it's not the money I want."

She reached for the blanket and pulled it up to cover her chest. "I want you to leave."

I ran my tongue over my bottom lip, then nodded in her direction. "We have unfinished business."

"The hell we do. You rescued me. I'm grateful. You want to get paid? Talk to my father. I have nothing to do with it."

My gaze traveled slowly over her body. "This isn't about your father or the money he owes me. This is about you and me."

Her eyes narrowed. "There is no you and me."

"I've had my cock deep inside of you, babygirl. Don't act like there is nothing between us."

She shifted on the bed as she clutched at the blanket. "You don't have to be so coarse. We had sex. That's all. It was no big deal. It didn't mean anything."

I winked as I reached down to grab my hard cock through my jeans. "Oh, trust me, baby, it was a *big* deal, and it did mean something."

She could try to blow it off as nothing, but I didn't believe her. She had been a virgin. I was the first man to claim her. The first to feel her tight pussy grip my cock. It fucking meant something—to both of us.

"Well, even if it did, it's over. I don't date Russians. So get out."

I smirked. "It's cute you think all I want to do is date you, and it's far from over, Katia."

"My name is Katie."

"Your name is Katia, and you are as full-blooded Russian as I am. You share the same hot passions and have the same fierce spirit. Stop denying your heritage. Stop denying what's between us."

She dropped the blanket and leaned toward me on her knees. "Are you deaf? There is no us!"

I whipped the belt from my jeans' belt loops. "I guess I'm just going to have to prove it to you."

She leaned back. "I'll scream."

I reached behind me, pulled out my Glock, and engaged the slide, chambering a bullet. I lifted it high, then placed it within reach on the top of her bureau. "Go ahead. First person through that door gets a bullet between the eyes."

She gasped.

I nodded. "Lie down on your stomach and pull your pajama shorts down."

"You can't be serious."

"Do I look like I'm joking?"

"Luka, I—"

"Do as I say. Now!"

She jumped and slid down the headboard. She turned onto her stomach. Her body stilled.

"Pull down your shorts and panties. Let me see those cute dimples of yours."

She sniffed as she swiped at a tear. Her arms trembled as she pushed her silk pajama shorts and a pair of light blue lace panties down to the tops of her thighs.

I folded my leather belt in half as I approached the bed. I used the belt to caress her skin. "You were a very bad girl, Katia. You should not have run away from me like that."

"You didn't give me a choice."

I continued to caress her skin. "You always have a choice. You chose to disobey me. Now you need to be punished. For your own safety, I need you to understand there are consequences for disobedience."

Her body trembled.

I stepped back and raised my arm.

Katia let out a yelp and curled into a fetal position.

I lowered my arm. "Don't make me tie you to the bed."

With a whimper, she resumed her position.

This time I didn't hesitate. I brought my heavy leather belt down on the soft curve of her ass.

Katia cried out before burying her head in her pillow to muffle her scream.

She took my threat of shooting anyone who dared disturb us seriously. Good, because I fucking meant it. I wouldn't hesitate to kill the first person who tried to interfere between me and Katia.

I raised my arm and spanked her with the leather strap a second and third time. Her butt cheeks clenched before each strike. A move I knew would only increase the pain of her punishment. I angled the belt to strike her upper thighs before returning to her plump ass. With each strike, Katia cried into her pillow.

Finally, she raised her tearstained face to me. "Please, it hurts."

I leaned over and stroked her wet cheek. "It's supposed to hurt. You were a bad girl."

"I'm sorry. I won't do it again."

"I need to make sure of that."

I raised my arm and spanked her ass several more times with my belt. Her skin glowed a bright cherry red as Katia kicked her legs and cried out in pain.

I was not striking her as hard as I could under the circumstances. I suspected this punishment had more warmed up her skin than caused any truly deep pain. "Spread your legs."

She didn't respond.

I struck her ass with my belt. "Spread your legs."

She sniffed into her pillow and opened her legs. I placed a hand between her smooth thighs and fingered her pussy. It was silky wet with arousal. "I think my baby is protesting a little too much."

Katia lifted up her head. Her bottom lip thrust out in a pout. "Am not! It fucking hurts."

I pulled off my shirt and kicked off my boots. I reached for the zipper of my jeans. "I'm going to show you hurt."

Her eyes widened. She started to rise.

"Stay right where you are," I ordered.

I pulled off my jeans and approached her bed naked, my heavily engorged cock swinging between my legs. Her bright blue eyes focused on it. I was pleased to see the fear leap within their ocean blue depths.

Reaching between her legs, I pulled her pajama shorts and panties off her.

Her bed was small and narrow. I slid in next to her and placed my hands on her hips to raise her over me. "Straddle my hips."

Not having a choice, Katia placed one knee on either side of my hips. I could feel the heat of her punished skin on the tops of my thighs.

She stared down at my stomach where my cock rested. "You can't fit that thing inside of me."

I smiled. "I did before."

She shook her head. "Impossible."

"Hold my cock."

She hesitated a moment before finally grasping its length. Her small hand was cool against the hot skin of my shaft. I lifted her by the hips. "Lower yourself down on me."

"Luka, I can't—"

"Baby, my cock is hard enough to pound nails and my patience is thin. Either put me inside of you, or I'm going to flip you back onto your stomach and pound into you until I make you scream."

She raised my cock upright between her legs. The soft wet entrance of her pussy teased the head. With excruciating slowness, she lowered herself halfway down onto my shaft.

Her breath came in shallow gasps as she raised herself back up and then lowered her hips again. I watched as her body opened to accept the thick girth of my cock. It was a beautiful sight.

"That's it, baby. Take my cock."

"It's starting to hurt."

"It's only halfway in. Keep pushing down."

"I can't."

"Yes, you can."

She bit her lip and clenched her ass cheeks as she pushed down a few more inches. Her fingernails clawed at my stomach as she leaned forward in an attempt to ease the pressure. Jesus, she was tight. Curled tendrils teased my nipples as her hair cascaded down around her face. I couldn't wait to gather it into my palm and yank hard as I pushed my cock down her willing throat.

I opened my legs, pushing the edges of my thighs against her own, forcing her legs to open wider. My cock slipped in another inch.

"Oh, God! It's too much. I'm going to tear," she cried out as her nails dug into my flesh.

"Trust me, baby."

I tightened my grip on her waist and surged my hips upward, completely impaling her.

Katia cried out.

I refused to relent. I moved my hips, thrusting in deep. Using the weight of her own body against her.

Katia's fingernails dug deep into my shoulders. "It hurts."

I reached around and grasped her ass, using the sting of her punished skin to my benefit.

Her torso snapped back as she opened her mouth on a gasp.

Snatching at her wrists, I flung her arms to the side as I reached for the collar of her pajama top. In one motion, I wrenched it open, sending the pearl buttons scattering. I palmed her full breasts as her body bounced on top of mine from the force of my thrusts.

After pinching her nipples to get them nice and hard, I returned my hands to her hips. I lifted her body up slightly only so that I could increase the power of my thrusts. As I pounded into her, I reveled in how her beautiful breasts bounced and swung with each thrust.

Looking between us, I watched as my shaft glistened in the low light from her arousal. The wetter she got, the easier it became to slide in deep.

I shifted my right hand to flatten my palm over her lower abdomen. I used the tip of my thumb to tease her clit, rubbing in counterclockwise circles. Her pussy clenched as her orgasm neared.

Katia threw her head back, the motion pushing her breasts forward. "Oh, God, I'm coming."

I pressed harder with my thumb, increasing the pace.

Katia wrapped her small hand around my wrist, holding my hand against her body as her mouth opened on a silent scream.

Burying myself deep inside her sweet pussy, I lurched upward. I wrapped my arms around her slight body and held her close as she came. My mouth latched onto her nipple, sucking and biting as I felt wave after wave crest over her body. A fine sheen of sweat formed over her chest and shoulders, giving her skin a salty tang as I licked and laved at her breasts.

Her head fell down on my shoulder as her body relaxed against mine.

I leaned back, taking her with me. I held her body prone over mine as I raised my knees and propped my feet against the mattress. I lifted my hips and plowed into her tight entrance. Feeling my own release build, I thrust hard and fast. "Fuck, baby. I'm coming," I breathed against her hair.

Her stupor left her. Katia lifted up her torso. "Pull out. You have to pull out."

I ignored her and continued to thrust.

"Luka, I'm not on birth control."

"I know."

I thrust in and came, shooting my seed deep inside her body.

Katia struggled against my embrace.

I flipped our bodies and pinned her underneath me. I thrust several more times for good measure.

"Take it out! Take it out, please."

"No."

I rested my forearms on either side of her head, determined to stay buried in her body until my seed hopefully took hold. I didn't want a drop of come to escape down her precious inner thighs.

A tear rolled down her cheek. "Why are you doing this?"

"Because I've decided to keep you."

"Keep me?"

"Yes, keep you."

"You can't *keep me*. I'm not some possession you can just claim."

I kissed her lips. "And yet that is precisely what I'm doing."

CHAPTER 16

Katie

"Will that be all?" asked the pharmacy cashier.

I adjusted my large sunglasses and nodded.

The moment she finished ringing up my purchase, I snatched the bag to my middle and practically ran out of the store. Brooklyn was waiting for me at a café around the corner. I'd told her I wanted to run into the pharmacy to grab a new bottle of nail polish.

Another lie.

As I crossed the opening to an alley, a hand reached out, wrapping around my upper arm and yanking me to the side. My body hit the brick wall a few feet inside the alley. Shocked, I tilted my head back to stare into the furious face of Luka.

"Are you following me?"

"Yes," he answered without hesitating.

I sputtered, "Well, knock it off."

"No."

He reached for the plastic shopping bag I was holding. I pushed it behind me. Luka raised a single eyebrow before reaching behind me. Our game of keep-away was brief with Luka being the obvious winner.

He opened the bag and pulled out a Plan B box. "What the fuck is this, Katia?"

I reached for the box, but he raised his arm out of my reach. "My name is Katie and it's none of your fucking business."

"Your name is Katia, and the fuck it isn't my business."

I placed my hands on my hips. "Listen, you big gorilla. I have plans for my future and they don't include having your baby."

He leaned his forearm against the brick, caging me in. "Then I guess I'm just going to have to try harder to convince you otherwise."

My stomach did backflips at the thought of what he meant by trying harder. Sex last night with him damn near killed me. I wasn't entirely sure the man hadn't rearranged my internal organs with that massive club he called a cock. There was no way this was just me being inexperienced. It wasn't like I lived in some convent virgin bubble. I knew what normal men looked like and what they did in bed and neither applied to Luka.

I came two more times last night before he finally let me rest. My cheeks burned at the memory of him watching me as he licked my pussy until I screamed with pleasure. The only reason why I got any sleep at all was because my tiny, narrow dorm bed was too small for the both of us.

Once again, I reached for the Plan B box. "Give it to me!"

He crushed the box with his fist. "Absolutely not. We'll talk about this more later. You are going to be late for class."

"How do you know my class schedule?"

"You'd be surprised how much I know about you, Katia."

"Katie. And I have plans for tonight."

His brow furrowed. "Your *plans* are to meet me at my hotel the moment you are done with classes at three p.m. today." He handed me a hotel key. "I have a penthouse suite at the Four Crowns two blocks away."

Seeing no other option, I took the key. "I can't. I have a ton of work to catch up on. I have to study tonight."

"You'll study at my hotel."

"I—"

"No is not an option." He nodded in the direction of the sidewalk. "Now go meet your friend and get to class."

"Fine, but I can't meet at three p.m. I have to go to the library first."

He nodded. "I don't want you walking around after dark. I'll pick you up at the library. When will you be finished?"

"Not until at least eleven."

He nodded.

As I turned to walk away, Luka called out, "Don't try anything, Katia. I'll be watching."

I stuck my tongue out at him and then took off running. When I arrived at the café, I was out of breath.

"What the hell?" asked Brooklyn.

"I, um, ran from a bee."

Lame. I internally rolled my eyes. I really was absolute crap at this lying stuff. I would have made a terrible criminal if I had followed in my family's footsteps.

She looked at my empty hands. "Weren't you at the store?"

"They didn't have the shade I wanted. Hey, you know that party you mentioned?"

She clapped and bounced in her seat. "The one at Alpha Theta Delta?"

I took a sip of her iced mocha. "That's the one. I'm in."

"Shut up! I thought you said you had to study?"

I shook my head. "Changed my mind. Can you pick me up at the library when you're ready to go?"

Brooklyn leaned back in her chair. "I never thought I'd see the day that Saint Kathryn decided to grace a fraternity party with her exulted presence."

I gave her shoulder a playful shove. "Shut up. I'm not that bad."

She scoffed. "Name the last party you went to with me."

"There was that one in the school gym with the lukewarm sodas and stale popcorn."

"That was freshmen orientation."

I scrunched my nose. "Okay, so maybe I've been a little focused on school and our future plans."

"A little? Nuns have had more fun than you these last

four years. We only have a few more months before we graduate. I'm glad you're *finally* acting like a normal college student."

Perhaps I had been a bit cloistered these last few years. I was so afraid that someone would learn my secret that I had kept a low profile on campus, only befriending a handful of people and never going out to frat parties or football games.

Luka.

Last night.

Him driving into me over and over again as I clawed his stomach and chest.

The feel of his belt on my ass as he punished me for running away.

Jesus, I had to stop thinking about him.

I fanned my cheeks.

Brooklyn frowned as she looked down at her iced drink. "Are you okay? You're not allergic to something in this mocha, are you?"

My cheeks burned even brighter. "No, just overheated from that stupid run I just did."

She laughed. "I had no idea you were so deathly afraid of bees."

I shrugged. "Now you know." Dammit, I was a terrible liar *and* friend.

"You know, David is probably going to be at the party."

"David?"

"Yeah, you know. The business major who has been trying to get in your pants since sophomore year."

"Oh, yeah, that David."

"Yeah, that David. He's going to be there tonight. He's an Alpha Theta Delta."

I took another sip of her iced mocha. "Really?"

Maybe that was what I needed. Maybe Luka wasn't as godlike as I thought. Maybe it was just because I'd never given another guy a fighting chance. Now that I wasn't a virgin anymore there was no point in holding back. Maybe this party would be good for me.

Again, I thought of Luka.

He was going to be so freaking pissed when he showed up at the library and I wasn't there.

Well, so what?

Despite what he said, he didn't own me.

I was my own person, and I had every right to go to a party if I wanted to.

To hell with him.

* * *

I COULD FEEL eyes on me as I walked up the brick steps of the library. I looked around but couldn't see Luka or his motorcycle. Still, I knew if it wasn't him out there it was someone who worked for him. Just because I couldn't see them didn't mean they weren't watching me. I wasn't going to take any chances. For the first few hours, I sat at a table visible through a nearby window doing my work. I then made a big show of selecting some art history books and stacking them high at a more secluded interior table. I continued to do my work until Brooklyn arrived.

She handed me a bag with my clothes. "Tell me again why you're not just going back to your dorm to change?"

I unzipped the bag and pulled out the V-neck top and jeans. "I didn't want to waste time and make you wait." I went to the bathroom to change. I didn't usually wear a lot of makeup but tonight I put on a thick layer of liquid black eyeliner to create a dramatic cat eye and some matte red lipstick. When I returned, I surprised her again by suggesting we go out the side door.

Brooklyn frowned. "Why?"

Thinking quickly, I stated, "Because I want to stash my backpack and books in one of the lockers."

She rolled her eyes. "You're not going to have any fun if you are already planning on ditching the party and coming back to the library later."

"I'm not! Really. I just know I have to be back here early tomorrow so I might as well leave my stuff."

"Fine."

We exited via the lesser-used side door. It was a long shot, but my hope was that not going out the front and being in different clothes might buy me some time.

* * *

THE MUSIC from the frat party could be heard half a block away as we followed the stream of students making their way to the large, somewhat dilapidated house. It was an old mansion that had definitely seen better days. The white clapboard facade was peeling and more of a dirty gray. There were several old sofas on the porch and lawn, which was also littered with red Solo cups. An Alpha Theta Delta flag flew from one of the windows.

As we approached, there was a fraternity brother,

naked but for his boxers, his chest painted with Greek letters, standing on the roof of the porch yelling out obscenities as he greeted guests by pouring beer on their heads.

I turned to Brooklyn. "Tell me again about how I've been missing out on this crucial college experience."

She put her arm through mine and tugged me along. "Come on. It won't be that bad. We'll stay for a few drinks and leave."

My lips twisted into a smirk. "I should have brought my camera. This would make for a great *wildlife* photo exhibit."

We laughed as we ran past a stream of beer from overhead to cross the frat house threshold. The moment we entered the house it was wall-to-wall bodies.

Brooklyn grabbed my hand. "Come on!"

"What?"

"What?"

I shook my head. The music was so loud I couldn't hear a word she was saying. "I can't hear you."

"Yeah. You're right. Let's get some beer."

I tugged on her hand. "What?"

Brooklyn gestured to a back corner of the room. "The beer? It's over there."

We shouldered our way through the drunk and dancing crowd till we found the keg. One guy pumped while another doled out foamy red Solo cups of some cheap unnamed beer. I grabbed the cup Brooklyn offered me and took a sip, grimacing from the bitter taste. "It's warm."

Brooklyn looked at me. "What?"

"I said, the beer is warm!"

Brooklyn raised her left arm and swayed her hips. "Yeah. Great idea! Let's dance!"

I am in hell.

Brooklyn dragged me to the center of the room. It wasn't so much dancing as just rocking back and forth to the music. There wasn't much room for anything else.

A hand grabbed my hip as someone ground their hips against my ass. I looked over my shoulder and grimaced at the sweaty, acne-prone face that leered back at me. I pushed his hands off me and pushed my way to the other side of Brooklyn. Thank God I had at least changed into jeans and didn't have on my thin yoga pants. Somehow the thicker denim gave me a little more protection against all the groping hands.

Brooklyn laughed as she took a swig from her beer. "Isn't this great?"

I forced a smile. As I lifted my cup to my mouth, someone bumped me from behind. Cheap beer sloshed down my front, drenching my shirt straight through to my lace bra. "Fuck!"

Brooklyn covered her mouth as she stared at me with wide eyes. "Katie! Oh, no!"

I pulled the sodden shirt away from my skin. "At least the beer wasn't cold."

She nodded in agreement. "Yeah. At least the shirt was old."

I rolled my eyes.

Yup, this is definitely hell.

My mother used to tease me about my lack of friends and how I wasn't a typical teenager. Even in high school, I preferred to stay behind the lens of my camera rather than interact with humanity. At least now I knew I hadn't missed out on much from skipping all those teenage parties.

A hand brushed my hair aside from behind and spoke into my ear. "Do you need help, baby?"

My heart leapt.

Luka was here.

I knew I was probably in trouble, but at that moment I had never been so happy to see him.

I smiled as I turned to face him.

It wasn't Luka.

David towered over me. He looked down at my stained shirt and then leaned in close, saying into my ear, "I can get you a clean shirt."

The backs of his knuckles brushed my arm as he spoke.

I tried to pull away from his embrace, but the moving bodies wouldn't let me. "I'm fine."

Brooklyn pinched my side.

I rubbed the spot. "Ow!"

She leaned in. "Stop being a prude."

I stuck my tongue out at her before turning back to David. I didn't know why I was hesitating. He was tall and handsome, and I already knew he was interested in me. Wasn't this what I'd come here for? To prove that Luka meant nothing to me?

David leaned in again. This time his mouth brushed my neck as he spoke. "Come on, baby. Come with me upstairs."

I felt nothing. None of the stomach flips or breathless emotions I felt when Luka called me baby.

I took a large swig of my beer.

Stop thinking about Luka. The man is a Russian and a criminal. He's completely out of the question for anything even remotely long-term.

I needed to remember my promise to myself. No Russian men! No ties to my family.

David was nice and a college student like me. He was an appropriate guy for me to be with. He probably didn't own a gun or a motorcycle or even know who the fuck the yakuza were. I needed to give him a chance.

Unwilling to shout over the crowd, I just nodded.

I glanced at Brooklyn over my shoulder as David led me away.

He elbowed his way through the crowd until we were at the bottom of the staircase. I pulled back slightly as he walked up the first few steps. He yanked on my arm. I stumbled, but started to climb the stairs.

We walked down a long, narrow hallway. On either side were just a series of wooden doors, some with stickers and posters, others bare. David stopped at the last door on the right. He unlocked it and turned on the light before motioning me inside.

I bit my lip as I crossed the threshold. The room was a mess. Dirty clothes were piled on the floor and on the bed. There were at least three half empty pizza boxes scattered about and both the desk and bureau were covered with crushed beer cans.

I turned to face him. "This was a mistake. I'm fine, really. It's practically dried already."

David leaned against the door, closing it. He reached behind him.

I could hear the lock click into place.

His gaze traveled over my body, settling on my chest. "Take off your shirt."

CHAPTER 17

*L*uka

"God dammit," I roared before turning and punching a hole in my hotel room wall. "What the fuck do you mean she's gone?"

Despite his height and brutish appearance, the man quaked in the face of my anger. "She'd been at that table for hours without moving. I didn't think taking a leak and grabbing a smoke would be that big of a deal."

He was one of the hired guns I'd borrowed from Gregor Ivanov to keep an eye on Katia until I was certain she was out of danger from both the yakuza and her piece of shit father.

I pulled my gun and pressed the barrel under his jaw. "How about now?"

He raised his hands, palms out. "I get it. I fucked up. I'm sorry, boss."

I returned my gun to the holster behind my back. I gave him a shove toward the door. "Get out of my fucking sight."

I turned to the two remaining men in the room. One stepped forward. "What do you want us to do?"

"Get out there and fucking find her!" I ordered, rubbing the fist I'd just put through the wall.

This was my fault. I should never have trusted someone else to watch over her while I took care of some business for Dimitri. I had hoped my punishment last night and my warning today had finally gotten through to her that the rules of the game had changed. She was no longer free to do as she pleased. She was under my protection, which meant she needed to follow my rules.

Apparently, I hadn't made myself clear earlier.

I wouldn't make that same mistake again.

I tucked an extra magazine clip into my back jeans pocket, grabbed my motorcycle keys, and headed out the door.

* * *

It didn't take long to find out the largest party on campus was at the Alpha Theta Delta frat house. It seemed like an unlikely place for Katia to go but I had already searched her dorm, the darkrooms in the Arts & Culture building, and the library. I was running out of options. If she wasn't at this frat party, I was going to call in reinforcements and turn this campus into a motherfucking war zone until I found her. At least so far, there was no evidence she had been kidnapped again. As far as I could tell, she deliberately snuck out of a side entrance of the library to avoid detection.

I would be having a very detailed… and painful… conversation about that with her as soon as I found her.

Bypassing someone puking on the front lawn, I headed for the front steps. A scrawny college student tried to stop me at the entrance. "Wow, dude, how old are you? This party is for hot chicks and frat brothers only."

I grabbed him by the T-shirt and slammed him against the wall. My eyes narrowed. "What did you just say to me?"

The kid's eyes popped out of his head. "Go on in, dude. Help yourself to the free beer."

I entered the house. It was chaos. Just a sea of drunken bodies swaying to an annoying pounding that I assumed most would call music. I shoved people out of my way as I searched over their heads for Katia. She was nowhere in sight.

Finally, after several minutes, I spotted her friend Brooklyn.

As I started in her direction, a blonde female stepped in front of me. She placed her hand on my chest. "Oh, my God, are all your tattoos real?"

I ignored her and tried to step past. She latched on to my arm as she swayed against me. Her words were slurred as she said, "Hey, where are you going? Don't you want to dance with me?"

I grabbed her by the shoulders and set her to the side. I continued in my path toward Brooklyn. She turned her back on me, swaying to the music as I approached. I tapped her on the shoulder. When she turned to face me, her eyes widened as she looked me up and down. "Where is Katia?" I shouted over the music.

Her nose scrunched up. "Who?"

"Katia!" I repeated before saying, "Katie! I'm looking for Katie."

Her eyes narrowed. "Who are you?"

"A friend."

Brooklyn crossed her arms while still holding her red Solo cup of beer. "I know all her friends and you're not one of them."

All this shouting and arguing was a waste of time. I grabbed her around the upper arm and dragged her to the back of the house. We walked through a swinging door into a mostly deserted kitchen. I motioned with my head to the few stragglers. "Get out."

Brooklyn broke free. "Hey! Who do you think you are?"

"I'm Katia... dammit, Katie's friend. Where is she?"

Brooklyn placed her hands on her hips. "I'm not telling you."

I rose to my full height and stepped toward her. She backed up. I continued following her until I had her pressed against the wall. I leaned in. "I don't know what she has told you, if anything, but Katie is my... girlfriend."

I hated that word.

It is so prosaic and American.

She isn't my girlfriend.

She is mine.

Fucking mine.

It was as simple as that.

Girlfriend was transient. It implied we were together

because it was convenient or fun for the moment. It did not fully capture how I felt about Katia or our relationship. This wasn't some bullshit flowers and chocolates on Valentine's Day and dates on Saturdays relationship. This was an all-consuming need to have her by my side, under my protection, every minute of every day until I was cold and dead in my grave and even then, I would continue to haunt her until she joined me in the afterlife. No, girlfriend was too stupid and simple of a word.

Wife.

That is a better word.

Brooklyn covered her mouth as she laughed. "Oh, my God! That little sneak! I knew that story about her being in the hospital was bogus. So tell me all the details! How did you meet? How long have you been dating? Did you sweep her away for some romantic getaway last week? Oh, my God! I can't wait to give her shit for not telling me about you! I can't believe she let me try and hook her up with that idiot David when she had *you*!"

Her ramblings were just noise until I heard the name David.

My eyes narrowed. "David? Who the fuck is David?"

Brooklyn pressed her lips together and looked away.

I pounded the wall. She jumped. "Who the fuck is David?"

Brooklyn shrugged. "He's just this guy. I'm sure she's not cheating on you. You see, someone spilled beer on her and David offered to give her one of his shirts."

A bright red glow of rage was cutting off my peripheral vision. "Where are they?"

Brooklyn scrunched up her face again and pointed to the ceiling. "Upstairs in his room," she squeaked out.

I turned and left the kitchen. Shoving bodies aside, I stormed up the stairs. There was a long corridor of closed doors. "Katia? Katia!"

I couldn't hear anything over the music and crowd below.

Turning to the first door, I kicked it open. The room was empty. I kicked the door across from it open.

"Hey!" called out an annoyed male.

I walked into the room and flicked on the lights. The man was on the bed on top of someone. I grabbed the back of his shirt and flung him across the room. The female sat up, holding her top to her breasts. It wasn't Katia.

I turned and left, ignoring the male's outraged response.

I kicked open a third and fourth door. More of the same.

Several frat brothers approached me from the end of the hallway. One of them spoke up. "You need to leave. Now."

I kicked open another door. "I'm not leaving until I find what I came here for."

One of the frat brothers charged me. I balled my hand into a fist and laid him out. He fell unconscious to the floor. "Anyone else want to stop me?"

The boys grabbed their friend under the arms and dragged him with them as they backed away.

I kicked the last door on the right open.

The first thing I saw was Katia's pale face.

She was standing on the bed, a baseball bat raised over her head.

David approached me. "What the hell, dude! This is my room. Get the fuc—"

I grabbed him by the throat and walked forward.

Katia called out, "Luka, no!"

I ignored her. As we reached the windows, I shoved David through the bedroom window on the right. The glass shattered around us as he stumbled back over the sill.

David clawed at my arm as he dangled from the second story window. "Pull me back in! Pull me in!"

I could barely get the words out through my clenched jaw. "You touched what's mine."

David's eyes widened as his voice went up an octave. "I didn't touch her, man. I swear."

Katia pleaded with me. "Luka, please. He didn't touch me. I'm okay."

She placed a calming hand on my shoulder. I looked down into her beautiful blue eyes. I didn't believe her. I had a flash of what might have happened if I had taken just a few more minutes to find her.

I tightened my grip around his throat. All the color left David's face as his grip slackened.

Police sirens wailed out down the street.

I pulled David's limp body back inside and dropped him to the floor with the rest of the trash.

I turned to Katia. I pulled the bat from her grasp and tossed it aside.

I leaned down and swept her into my arms. She clung to my neck as she buried her head against my shoulder.

The crowd of onlookers parted as I carried her out of the room and down the stairs.

Downstairs was completely empty; the drunk college students had scattered the moment they heard the police sirens. I kicked aside the piles of empty Solo cups and crushed beer cans as I carried her outside. Two police officers approached me, guns drawn. I didn't even stop at their command. "I am Luka Siderov, friend of Gregor Ivanov. If you have a problem, call him."

The police lowered their weapons. Allowing me to pass, they turned their attention to the frat brothers who were loudly complaining about their broken window and unconscious friend.

I overheard one officer's response. "Shut the hell up! Do you have any idea who that guy was? You're lucky he didn't rip your friend's head off."

As we approached my bike, Katia lifted her head. "Am I in a lot of trouble?"

I looked down at her pale face and growled, "Princess, you have no idea just how much trouble you are in right now."

CHAPTER 18

Katie

LUKA PUT me down near his motorcycle. I pointed down the street. "My dorm is only two buildings down. I can just go—"

Luka got on the bike and wrapped his hands around my waist. He lifted me high, forcing me to straddle his hips as he lowered me onto the bike in front of him. "The only place you are going is with me."

He started up the bike and took off into the night. At first, I tried not to hold on to him but gave up after the first turn. I wrapped my arms around his waist and leaned my head against his shoulder. It was a fast ride. The Four Crowns Hotel was just on the edge of campus. He left the motorcycle out front and escorted me inside. I caught the front desk clerk's curious gaze, but one look from Luka and he immediately averted his eyes.

My cheeks burned. I was sure the clerk had all sorts of salacious ideas considering Luka was so much older than me. We stepped into the elevator and Luka chose the penthouse.

I twisted the ring on my finger. "That clerk thinks I'm some kind of escort."

"So?"

"So? So, I'm not used to people mistaking me for a hooker."

Luka tilted his head and gazed down at me. "If you didn't dress like one, people wouldn't think that."

With an outraged gasp, I looked down at my outfit. The beer had loosened the V-neck collar of my shirt, causing it to sag so low the top of my lace bra was in full view. My eyes widened as I grasped the fabric with my fists. "Why didn't you tell me?"

Luka smirked as he placed a hand on my lower back and led me out of the elevator and down the hallway. "I was a little busy not tearing the head off the man I found you with."

I narrowed my eyes. "You make it sound like you found me naked in bed. I wasn't going to do anything with that guy."

Luka's gray eyes were a piercing bright silver as he looked down at me. "And that is the only reason he's still alive right now."

A shiver rippled over my body. I knew those weren't just words. He was fucking serious. If David had managed to get my shirt off and get me on the bed like he intended, Luka would have probably killed him right there and then. Witnesses be damned.

He opened the double doors leading into the spacious penthouse suite. I stepped past the marble entryway and into the living room. Luka crossed the room to the bar. He poured himself a drink and drained the glass before pouring himself another one.

I stood in the center of the room, nervously twisting the silver band ring on my finger as I stared at his back. Out of the corner of my eye, I noticed the massive hole in the hotel wall. It was the size of a fist. Oh, fuck.

Finally, he spoke, although he didn't turn around to face me. "Go get a shower. You reek of cheap beer. And wash all that fucking makeup off your face."

"I'm fine. I'll just get one when I—"

He slammed his glass down onto the bar. "God dammit, Katia. For once, do as I fucking say."

I ran across the room to the closest bedroom. I passed the massive king-size bed and went straight into the bathroom. I closed and locked the door. Not that that would do any good if Luka wanted to come in. I stood in the center of the bathroom for several minutes, unsure of what to do. I had very little chance of sneaking out of this hotel room without Luka seeing me. Even if I did manage it, he'd probably just show up at my dorm room even angrier than he was now... if that was possible.

Seeing no other option, I pulled the stained and still damp shirt over my head. I unhooked my bra as I kicked off my sneakers. I started the shower before pulling down my jeans and panties.

I let out a long sigh as I stepped in under the hot stream of water. After lathering my hair, I used the pearl iridescent soap to scrub my body and the makeup off my face.

Stepping out of the shower, I slipped into one of the large, fluffy robes the hotel offered after drying off. As much as I hated to admit it, I did feel better. It felt good to wash away the smell of that frat house.

And, hopefully, it had given Luka time to calm down.

I tightened the belt of the robe as I crossed the bedroom threshold back into the living room area. Luka had changed out of his clothes and into a pair of gray sweatpants. His muscled and tattooed back was to me as he sipped from his drink and stared out the massive floor-to-ceiling windows. The view was of downtown Worthington and the mountains in the distance, although all you could see now was shadowed outlines and a few twinkling lights in the darkness.

I cleared my throat. "Listen, I'm sorry about tonight."

Luka didn't respond or turn around.

I played with the edge of the terrycloth belt. "It's not like I did anything wrong. I'm in college. College students go to frat parties all the time."

Still no response.

"It was stupid of me to go up to that guy's room. I've never done anything like that before. I just wanted to prove..."

Luka turned. "Wanted to prove what?"

I blinked. I was seriously regretting the deeply honest and super embarrassing thing I almost admitted to. "N-nothing."

His eyes narrowed. "Wanted to prove what, Katia?"

"You were my first and I just wanted to see—"

He clenched his jaw so tight, I could see a tic twitch near his right eye. He breathed heavily through his nose several times before finally speaking. When he did his voice was hoarse and low with anger. "Are you telling me you almost fucked that piece of shit boy to prove—what? That what we have is nothing special?"

That was precisely what I was trying to prove, but I'd be damned if I'd admit it to him.

I opened my mouth several times to speak but couldn't come up with a believable lie.

He took a long sip from his glass. His gaze moved over me, slowly and methodically. "Take your robe off."

My inner thighs clenched together. Oh, God. I both wanted and dreaded whatever was about to happen. The man both fascinated and terrified me and I had never seen him as angry as he was tonight.

"Luka, we need to talk about—"

He growled, "Take. Off. Your. Robe."

Afraid of making it worse if I didn't obey, with shaking hands I undid the belt and pulled the robe off my shoulders. It dropped to the floor around my feet. I used my arms to cover my breasts and between my legs.

Luka turned to the side and splashed more whiskey into his glass before facing me. "Get on your knees."

My eyes filled with tears. "Please, don't do this."

"Get on your knees, Katia."

Swiping at the tears that were falling down my cheeks with the back of my hand, I lowered myself to my knees.

Luka stared at me over the rim of his glass as he took another long sip.

The only sound in the room was the rattle of the ice in his glass and my own shallow breaths.

His wolf-like eyes glinted in the soft light of the room. "Now crawl to me."

I swallowed a sob. I squeezed my eyes shut as a wave of humiliation crested over my body.

"I'm waiting, Katia."

I opened my eyes. With no other option, I lowered my hands to the carpeted floor and crawled across the room. I was acutely aware of my bare back and ass being on full display as my heavy breasts swung between my arms with each forward movement.

I kept my eyes cast downward as I crawled to him. I stopped at his bare feet. I tilted my head up slightly, but my first view was of his heavy cock perfectly outlined in his sweats as it rested along his inner thigh. I swallowed as I hastily lowered my gaze.

He placed a hand under my chin and raised my head. He said nothing. Only stared. He then rubbed the pad of his thumb over my lower lip. Back and forth. Before pushing it inside, forcing my mouth open. I swirled my tongue around his thumb as it invaded my mouth.

Luka growled in response. "Pull out my cock."

I rose up on my knees, gingerly pulled down the waistband of his sweatpants, and reached in to grasp his shaft. I pulled back the moment I touched it. His skin was so hot. He was so fucking big and hard.

He grabbed my hand and forced it back inside his pants. His cock sprang free. My hand looked small and pale as I tried to wrap my fingers around the thick width.

"Now open your mouth."

"Please. I've never. I don't know how."

He stroked my lower lip with his thumb again. "Good, another virgin hole. Now open."

His cock was right at my eye level. The head was large and bulbous. It was so engorged it looked almost purple. I could feel his shaft pulse and move under my fingers. I opened my mouth, but then closed it. I tightened my lips between my teeth as I shook my head.

Luka snatched a fistful of my hair. He leaned down. "Open your mouth and suck my cock or I'm going to flip you onto the bed and plow into your virgin ass next."

My eyes widened. Oh, God.

My lips trembled as I opened my mouth. I stretched out my tongue and licked the tip. He tasted salty. I licked him a second time, swirling my tongue around the edge of his head.

Luka tugged on my hair.

I sniffed as I closed my eyes and tried to take him into my mouth. I could only fit the head and an inch of the shaft past my lips before my mouth was full. My tongue shifted under him.

"You're going to have to do better than that, babygirl."

Luka pushed on the back of my head, driving himself deeper into my mouth. The head of his cock hit the back of my throat and I gagged. I wrenched my head backward. He pushed again. I placed my hands on the tops of his thighs to try to pull back. Luka pulled on my hair harder. Widening his stance, he pushed on the back of my head till I felt his cock slip deeper down my throat. I couldn't breathe. Before I could panic, he pulled out. I gasped for air, but after getting a gulp, he pushed his cock past my lips. This time he thrust several times, bruising the back of my throat as I struggled to move my tongue out of the way of his thick shaft.

He pulled out again.

I breathed in, then begged, "Please. I can't do this."

"You can and you will. Maybe this time you'll learn to listen."

He tried to push his cock back into my mouth, but I turned my head. "I'm sorry I disobeyed you."

Luka smiled. "You will be. You're about to learn. Bad girls get skull fucked when they disobey."

He yanked on my hair so hard I gasped in pain. The moment my mouth opened he thrust inside. My shoulders shook as I choked on his cock. He pulled back and thrust again. This time he slipped past the resistance in the back of my throat to slide down it.

My lips were stretched thin around the wide base as he ruthlessly pushed in further.

Just when I thought I couldn't hold my breath any longer, he pulled out.

Keeping his hand in my hair, he took a sip from his drink as he watched me choke and suck in precious air. "Open," he demanded.

With a whimper, I obeyed.

My teeth scraped the bottom of his shaft as he pushed in again. My jaw ached as I tried to please him by moving my tongue as I sucked in my cheeks. Luka groaned. I felt a twisted sense of satisfaction.

He placed his glass on a nearby table and shifted his stance.

He used his grip on my hair to move me backward until my body hit the back of the sofa.

Luka placed his palms on the top of the sofa as he leaned over me. "Now comes your real punishment."

A wave of terror rippled down my spine. "No, I—"

He thrust inside my mouth. My head was trapped between his muscled thighs and the back of the sofa. He went in deep, giving no quarter. He pulled back and thrust again, using my mouth for his own pleasure. Spittle formed at the corners of my mouth as I struggled to swallow his shaft. My lips were bruised and swollen as they were pressed against the sharp edges of my teeth. He pushed past my gag reflex and shoved his cock deep down my throat. I tilted my head back as far as I could to try to ease the pressure.

I struggled to breathe through my nose as I clasped the fabric of his pants in a fruitless effort to hold him back.

He thrust in deep. "That's it, baby. Open that throat for me."

I relaxed my throat and followed the rhythm of his thrusts. I could feel him getting harder as he increased the pace. He let out a guttural groan as he pushed in so deep the hair around the base of his cock tickled my nose.

Before I knew what was happening, he pulled free of my mouth and picked me up. He carried me into the bedroom and tossed me down onto the center of the bed. "Punishment's over. I need to taste this pussy."

Luka straddled my face with his knees as he placed his head between my legs.

"Oh, God! Wait! What?" I was so shocked I couldn't get out the words, which was a good thing because he pushed down with his hips and thrust his cock back into my mouth the moment his tongue flicked my clit.

My hips thrust upward. He braced his elbows against the mattress and gripped my ass with his hands. He licked and laved at my pussy as he pushed his cock into my mouth. It was so fucking hot. I felt dominated and yet in control at the same time. Of course I knew about the sixty-nine position, I just never thought I'd be the type of girl to try it.

As scary as it was, Luka angrily fucking my mouth had completely turned me on. I was already wet and on the edge by the time he touched me with his tongue. It didn't take long for me to feel the building release of an intense orgasm.

I screamed around his cock as my hips shot off the bed.

Luka pulled free and flipped me around. He grabbed my legs and put them over his shoulders. "I'm not wasting a fucking drop," he warned before he plowed into me. He thrust several times before roaring his release.

He collapsed to my side before pulling me into his arms. He reached for a corner of the quilted bedspread and pulled it over our sweaty, naked bodies as we each struggled to catch our breath.

He wrapped his hand around my jaw and pulled my head to the side to face him. "Don't ever fucking disobey me again, babygirl."

I swallowed. "I won't."

He tightened his grasp for one terrifying moment, then released my jaw and used the backs of his fingers to stroke my cheek. "You don't understand how close I came to losing control. I don't want to hurt you, but I will if that is what it takes to get you to listen and obey."

I nodded, not knowing how to respond.

He leaned over and kissed my forehead. "Trust me, baby. You don't ever want to test me like that."

I shivered but with fear, not cold.

Luka wrapped his arms tightly around me.

He was a force of nature. A terrible, twisting tornado and I was now caught in the eye of his storm. There was no chance of a future for us. The problem was I now understood just how destructively ugly, and possibly deadly, the end would be.

CHAPTER 19

Katie

I AWOKE to the soft sound of Luka snoring behind me. His arm was wrapped around my waist. There was a small streak of sunlight peeking between the heavy blackout curtains. I shifted my hips and tried to slide out from under his arm.

His arm tightened around my waist. He rasped against my neck as he pulled me closer, "Where do you think you're going?"

I bit my lip. "I need to pee."

He squeezed me for a moment and then let me go.

I slid out of the bed and ran naked into the bathroom.

I flipped on the faucet and ran the water full blast to cover the sound of me peeing. I then placed a washcloth under the tap and lifted it to my face. The soaked cloth cooled my heated cheeks. Pulling it down, I stared at my reflection. It took a moment for me to even recognize myself. My hair was a tangled riot of curls around my face. My eyes had a bright, almost feverish glow to them and my lips looked like I was trying to out-lip a Kardashian. They were still swollen and a deep dark pink from the blowjob I had given Luka last night. Although blowjob seems too tame of a word for what we did.

I still couldn't believe what we did… what he did… what I did! It was all a blur of mouths and lips and other things. I pressed the cold cloth to my cheeks as they started to warm again.

It was okay.

Everything was okay.

I was just going to get dressed and leave here with as much dignity as I could muster. There was plenty of time to curl up in the fetal position under a mountain of covers and hash over all the humiliating things I actually enjoyed about last night.

I wrinkled my nose as I picked my dirty jeans off the floor. With a grimace, I slipped one leg in, then the other. Realizing I forgot my panties, I swiped them off the floor and shoved them into my pocket. I did the same with my bra before pulling the disgusting shirt I wore last night over my head. God, I hoped that nasty little busybody clerk wasn't still manning the front desk when I did the walk of shame past him.

I took a deep breath and opened the bathroom door.

Luka was still in bed. He turned his head at the sound and frowned. He tossed the blankets off himself.

I held out my hands. "No need to get up. Sleep. I'm just going to see myself out."

Without saying a word and uncaring that he was naked as a jaybird, he stormed toward me. He grabbed the shirt I had just put on and ripped it over my head.

"Hey!" I protested.

He picked me up around the waist and tossed me back onto the bed. He then grabbed my ankles and pulled the jeans off my legs. He gathered up both items and calmly walked over to the balcony door.

I sat up. "Luka! Don't you dare!"

He opened the balcony door and tossed my clothes over the railing.

"Oh, my God! My clothes!"

He then closed the door and got back into bed. He pulled me down next to his side and tossed the blanket over us again.

I tried to rise several times, but he kept pulling me back down. "I can't believe you just did that! Those were my only clothes!"

"Go back to sleep. It's still early."

"I don't want to go back to sleep. I want to leave."

"Not happening."

"You can't keep me prisoner."

Luka pulled the covers off me. "Go ahead. Leave."

I scurried back under the covers. "You know I can't leave without any clothes."

He closed his eyes as he draped an arm around me. "All part of my evil plan."

"This isn't funny."

"I'm not joking. I have nothing but evil intentions toward you and this tight little body of yours." He then pinched my ass.

"Ow! You're impossible."

"So they tell me."

With a huff, I settled back down. Soon the comforting warmth of his body lulled me back to sleep.

* * *

I AWOKE to the smell of bacon.

I shifted only to feel cold sheets at my side. Luka was no longer in bed with me. It was strange how empty it felt without him.

Luka strolled into the bedroom wearing his usual pair of gray sweatpants and eating a strip of bacon. My gaze traveled down to his semi-hard cock that swung like a heavy pendulum every time he took a step. He followed my gaze and winked. "I thought you might be too sore, but I'm game if you are."

My eyes widened at being caught staring at his junk. "No! I'm good."

He sat on the edge of the bed and held out the second half of his slice of bacon. I tried to take it from him, but he pulled back. He raised an eyebrow and held it close again. Dutifully, I opened my mouth and allowed him to feed me the slice. The intimacy of the simple act startled me.

He stroked my cheek. "Come into the living room. Breakfast is ready."

Before I could wonder if I should wrap up in the blanket or try to wrench the sheet off the bed and use that, Luka returned to the bedroom with the robe I was wearing last night. I shyly took it from him and slid my arms into the sleeves before swinging my legs off the side of the bed and rising.

As we both walked into the living room, I gasped. "How many people are eating breakfast with us?"

He shrugged. "Just us."

There were two room service trolleys filled with trays and bowls. There was a pile of bacon, another of sausage, and yet another of ham. There was a small chafing dish of scrambled eggs as well as a bowl of poached. There had to be at least half a loaf of toasted bread in a basket. There was also a glass bowl filled with fresh fruit salad resting in a metal bowl filled with ice.

He sat at the small table in the breakfast nook area as he reached for a plate. "If you don't see anything you like, let me know and I'll call room service."

I sat next to him. "No. It's fine."

"What can I get you?" he asked as he held up the plate.

"Some eggs and some bacon and a little fruit."

He nodded and filled my plate high. He then fixed himself a plate and poured us both a cup of coffee from the carafe on the sideboard. We then ate in silence.

It was all so domestic.

It was freaking me out.

Breaking the silence, I said, "I need to get back to the library. I have a ton of work to do."

He frowned. "It's Saturday."

"I have a week's worth of homework to catch up on."

He nodded. He then turned and reached for his phone. The moment someone answered he started speaking in rapid-fire Russian. I knew the language better as a young child. As I got older, I refused to learn or speak it further, but I still remembered some words. I caught clothes, books, library, key.

When he hung up, I asked. "What was that about?"

"It's taken care of."

"What is taken care of?"

"Eat your breakfast."

With a frustrated sigh, I picked up my fork and speared a piece of cantaloupe. Something told me I should eat to keep up my strength around him.

Not a half hour later there was a discreet knock at the door. Luka answered. The man in the hallway handed him a stack of books, a duffel bag, and what looked suspiciously like my backpack.

"Is that my bag?"

Luka closed the door and deposited the items next to me on the sofa. The duffel bag was unzipped. I could see my college sweatshirt and a pair of silk pajama bottoms. "You had someone break into my dorm room? And how did you get my backpack? It was in a locked locker at the library."

He shrugged. "He unlocked it."

"This is not okay."

"You wanted clothes and your books to study. You have both now. Be happy." He kissed me on top of my head. "I'm going to shower. Don't try and leave."

I stuck my tongue out at his retreating back.

He chuckled as he walked into the bedroom. "I saw that."

The man really was part beast with eyes in the back of his head.

I truly wanted to spite him and up and leave while he

was in the shower. But I didn't. I changed into my soft sweatshirt and my hot-pink silk pajama pants. Then I curled up on the sofa with a small bowl of fruit salad next to me as I opened my laptop. I surveyed the stack of books that I'd checked out of the library yesterday, looking for the one I needed. There were also several I hadn't checked out.

I lifted up a leather-bound and gilt copy of *The Old Man and the Sea* by Ernest Hemingway.

Just then Luka returned. Fresh from a shower, he was now wearing a pair of black cotton pajama pants. "That one's mine."

He strolled over to the desk and picked up a pair of reading glasses. He then flopped down on the sofa near me and reached for the book.

"You're reading *The Old Man and the Sea*?"

He grinned. "I figured I would catch up on some classic American literature during my stay in America."

I turned back to my work, but it was hard to concentrate.

Luka quietly sat reading only a few feet away.

Seriously, was there anything sexier than a man reading? He hadn't shaved so he had a slight five-o'clock shadow on his jaw. His chest was bare, so all his colorful tattoos were on full display. Even his feet looked sexy as he propped them up on the coffee table, crossing them at the ankles. He had on a pair of simple black wire-rimmed reading glasses that made him seem even sexier as he calmly flipped each page as he finished reading it.

A beastly, tatted-up, mafia mercenary who rode a big scary motorcycle and killed people for a living was silently reading fucking Hemingway next to me while I did my schoolwork.

For the thousandth time, I glanced at him from under my lashes.

Luka didn't look up from his book. "If you keep looking at me like that, I'm going to take you into the bedroom, spread your legs, and fuck you senseless."

With a gasp, I turned my attention back to my own book. I scribbled a few notes in my notebook and made a notation on the document I had open on my computer. After several minutes, I couldn't help but glance at Luka again.

Luka slammed his book shut. "That's it."

He stood and grabbed my arm. He then pulled me onto his shoulder.

I playfully kicked. "No! Wait! I have homework!"

He slapped me on the ass as he carried me into the bedroom. "Good. Let's play naughty schoolgirl and the professor."

CHAPTER 20

Luka

"What are you doing?"

I watched as Katia pulled her ever-present digital camera out of her backpack.

She leaned back on the sofa as she lifted the camera to her face. "Nothing."

The camera clicked as she took several photos of me.

We had just finished making love for the third time that day. Katia had returned to her schoolwork, and I was at the nearby hotel desk at my own laptop. I was reviewing the details of a possible deal Dimitri and Vaska were putting together with a warlord in some rat-hole country.

The camera clicked again.

"Careful, my ugly face will probably break your lens," I teased.

Katia climbed off the sofa and approached me. She held up the camera and flipped through the images she had just taken. There were several close-up black-and-white images of me.

She nodded her head in approval. "You are extremely photogenic. I knew you would be with those wolf eyes and defined cheekbones."

I pulled her onto my lap and playfully batted my eyelashes. "I've always wanted someone to notice my *defined* cheekbones."

She laughed as she leaned back and took another photo. She then showed me the small screen. "I'm serious. You have a very arresting look. The camera loves you."

I leaned over and nibbled on her neck, making sure to lick the sensitive spot just below her ear. As I reached over to take the camera from her, she scrambled off my lap and flopped back onto the sofa. "Oh, no, you don't, I have to finish this project. I already missed the deadline. My photography professor only offered me an extension until Monday."

I closed my laptop and joined her. I looked at the screen of her laptop. There were several images of ballerinas in motion. They were entrancing. "You do amazing work."

She tilted her head down as she pushed a curl behind her ear. "You think so?"

"You captured the fluid movement of their arms and legs and costumes expertly."

She smiled. "Thank you. I'm kind of sentimental about photographing ballerinas. My mother wanted to be a ballerina. She would have been spectacular."

I frowned. "What happened?"

Katia shrugged as her features stiffened. Her voice was cold when she answered, "She met my father."

She began to shift to the right, placing some distance between us. It wasn't a physical wall but it felt like one.

I was having none of it.

I grabbed her laptop and tossed it onto the coffee table. I then snatched her around the waist and flipped her until she was trapped beneath the weight of my body.

I frowned down at her. "Don't do that."

She frowned back. "Don't do what?"

"You know damn well what. Don't lump me in with the likes of your asshole father. I'm nothing like him."

She turned her head to the side, avoiding my gaze. "I'm sure that's what my mother, Alina, thought when she first met my father, too. Then he ruined her life. He's the reason why she never became a professional ballerina. He refused to let her pursue her dreams."

"I would never stop you from pursuing your dreams, Katia. You have to know that."

She shoved at my chest, but I wouldn't budge. "I don't have to know anything. Besides, the point is moot. We are having some fun, nothing more. There's no future between us."

I snatched at her wrists and stretched them over her head. "How many times do I have to tell you… to show you… that I'm not going anywhere. You're mine, Katia, and I'm never letting you go."

She swiped at a tear that had rolled down her cheek. "I bet that's just what my father told my mother, and he was right. She only finally escaped him in death."

God fucking dammit. The next time I saw Egor Novikoff I was going to personally strangle him to death with my bare hands. In this moment I wanted nothing more than to see the light of life drain from that wretched old man's eyes for the hurt he'd caused Katia and her poor departed mother.

There was no point in arguing with her. Actions spoke louder than words. Over time, I would prove to her that I was nothing like her father. That I wanted nothing more than to see her happy, pursuing whatever dream she wished, as long as that dream included me at her side.

I meant what I said. She was mine and I wasn't going to let anything come between us, including her.

Maybe it was time I made this arrangement more permanent? With the way we were fucking, it was only a matter of time before she carried my child. Yes, it was past time I gave her and my possible future child the protection of my name.

I smiled down at Katia as I brushed her hair away from her face. "No more talk of depressing things. How about I run you a bubble bath and order up some of your favorite chocolate cake?"

She tried to hide a smile and failed. She sniffed as she wiped away the last of her tears. "Actually, that sounds nice."

As I rose from the sofa and crossed to the hotel phone, I pulled out my cell phone and sent a text to Gregor Ivanov. If I was going to plan a quick wedding to Katia, I would need to inform him and Mikhail and Damien of the trouble coming when Katia's father found out.

I watched as she rose from the sofa and crossed into the bedroom.

She was going to make me a beautiful wife—the sooner the better.

CHAPTER 21

*L*uka

I STROLLED into Gregor Ivanov's study.

He was on the phone but looked up and nodded. He then gestured to the samovar on the sideboard. I walked over and picked up a *podstakannik* and slipped a clear tea glass into it. I then lifted the ceramic teapot off the top of the urn and poured a generous amount into my glass. I twisted on the spigot to fill the glass with hot water. After adding a small amount of sugar, I turned to Gregor who was still on his phone call as he joined me at the sideboard. He poured some strong concentrated tea into his glass and followed it with hot water before taking a seat behind his desk.

As I waited for Gregor to finish his call, Damien strolled in.

He slapped me on the shoulder. "Luka Siderov! How have you been, my friend?"

I nodded. "Well, my friend."

"I hear you've been causing quite a bit of trouble both in Chicago and here since your arrival in America."

I shrugged as I took a sip of the strong tea. "Subtlety has never been my strong suit."

Damien laughed as he dropped into the chair next me. "Subtlety is boring and overrated. Just ask my wife."

I smiled. "How is Yelena?"

I had met them both when she was studying in Paris last year.

His eyes lit up. "She is well. Keeping me on my toes as always."

"Has she finished that fashion collection she was working on?"

"Yes. She's upstairs now with a small sewing crew working on the final dresses."

"She doesn't need a photographer to take photos of the clothes, does she?"

He raised a hand and shook his head. "I'm not sure. Did you want me to ask her?"

The idea of getting Katia some work pleased me. "Yes, please do. I know a talented photographer she should hire."

"This talented photographer doesn't happen to have blue eyes and terrible taste in men, does she?"

My eyes narrowed. "Yes, on both counts. Why else would she be with me?"

We both laughed.

Damien slapped me on the shoulder. "So it is official? You are going to join our leg-shackled ranks?"

Before I could answer, Gregor ended his phone call. "I wouldn't be so sure of that."

I frowned. "Tell me."

Gregor nodded to his cell phone. "That was one of my men reporting to me from Moscow. Apparently Egor Novikoff's kicking up a storm over you not returning his daughter to him after you rescued her."

"He can fuck right off."

Gregor sighed. "It's not that easy. He has the backing of Pavel Petrov. This could get messy."

"Do you have my back?"

"Always."

"Then there isn't a problem."

Damien leaned forward in his seat. "We need to secure Katia. If he hired Luka, he'll hire someone else to get her to Russia."

Gregor nodded. "True. We need to marry her off to a strong family who will protect her from the Novikoffs and Petrovs."

I cracked my knuckles. "I'm marrying her."

Gregor leaned back in his seat. "Luka."

My gaze narrowed. "No."

He persisted. "You have to listen to reason, my friend. You have no connections. No family. She is the only daughter of a powerful Russian family. We shouldn't waste her marriage. She should be married off to a family whose alliance we will most benefit from. A family with the manpower to keep her safe."

I stood and paced across the room. What Gregor said was true and it would be the sensible course of action. I had no parents or siblings. No real connections. For most, I was a ghost, a nightmare they called up in the middle of the night to handle their demons. Then by morning I was gone, and they could forget they had even turned to me for help. I was the worst possible choice of a husband for Katia. And yet, I had no intention of letting her marry anyone else.

My fingers curled into a fist. "I will keep her safe. No one would dare take her from me if she were my wife."

Gregor reached for the cigar box on his desk and took one out before turning it around to offer one to Damien and me. He clipped off the end and carefully lit it. "Think about this for a moment. Is this the smart play for both you and her? Are you ready to take on a wife? Is this what you truly want? If you're worried about the girl, we'll find someone honorable to marry her. I won't just toss her to the wolves."

I selected a cigar. Brushing aside his offer of a cutter, I bit off the end and spit it into the trash can by his desk. I flicked open my lighter and ran the flame under the rolled tobacco, heating it. I took my time, wanting to think about Gregor's question and not just respond out of pride or anger.

I trusted Gregor's judgment. He was an honorable man who was always good for his word. He would never take his anger at Egor out on the man's daughter. It wasn't his style. If he said he would find someone acceptable for Katia, he would.

The problem was Katia already had a man. Me.

I blew out a fragrant cloud of smoke. "I know this may

come as a surprise to both of you, but I'm not wavering. Katia is mine and I'll kill any man who tries to take her away from me."

Damien selected his own cigar. "This is going to get bloody."

Gregor leaned back in his chair and put his feet up on the desk. He blew a smoke ring. "Let it. The yakuza didn't put up any kind of real fight. They spoiled our fun."

Damien nodded absently. "True. It's been ages since we've killed anyone."

I laughed. "You're becoming old married men who sit by the fire and get fat."

Gregor pointed at me with his cigar. "Laugh it up. You're planning on joining our ranks soon."

Damien leaned over to tap his cigar in the ashtray. "And it needs to be soon. If we are going to pull this off, Katia needs to become your wife quickly. It would be even better if she were already carrying your child. Lock the whole thing up. Egor wouldn't be able to try and annul it."

I bit the cigar between my teeth as I winked at Damien. "Already working on it."

Gregor leaned forward. "We can have the wedding here. This weekend. Let's get it done."

Damien chimed in. "Yelena has a few wedding gowns in her collection. I'm sure she'll lend one to you for Katia to wear."

Gregor pressed the intercom button on his phone. "Samara, *malyshka*. Can you come to the study? I have a surprise for you." He then looked up at us. "She has been dying for some entertainment ever since the baby was born. This will be just the thing."

Damien pulled out his phone. "I'll text Mikhail and Nadia to make sure they don't make any plans for the weekend."

Gregor nodded. "Good idea. We'll keep it small. Mostly family. Send the message to both the Novikoffs and the Petrovs that we consider Luka family and he has our support."

I rose and stubbed out my cigar. "It is all settled then. Guess I better go inform the bride."

CHAPTER 22

Katie

I HAD SPENT the whole weekend with Luka. We read. We laughed. We ate. We made love.

It was amazing.

It was terrifying.

Sunday night, as he tucked me into his side as we prepared to sleep, I realized I was falling for him. I was falling for the Russian criminal with ties to my horrible criminal family.

This was a disaster.

Somehow, some way, I had to get far away from this man.

* * *

Brooklyn scowled at me as we met outside my classroom. "How come you didn't tell me you have a smoking hot boyfriend?"

I adjusted the strap on my backpack. "It's... complicated."

"What's so complicated? He's hot as hell and obviously loves you."

My head turned so quickly in her direction, I got a crimp in my neck. As I rubbed the pain away, I asked, "What makes you say that?"

"The way he was completely freaked out looking for you at the party the other night. I wish I had a guy who cared that much about me."

I continued to play with the strap on my backpack. "He was freaked out?"

She nodded. "Um, yeah! It was obvious he was really worried about you. I never would have pushed you to hang out with David if I knew you had a boyfriend."

I took her hand in mine. "It's my fault. It's all really new and I'm not sure how I feel about it, so I didn't want to say anything just yet. Plus, it's not like we were exclusive or anything."

"Yeah, you may want to tell him that. I was getting a hardcore *hands off she's mine* vibe from the dude."

Sounds like Luka.

We walked in silence for a few minutes. Finally, I couldn't resist asking, "You really think he loves me?"

Brooklyn cast me a side-eyed glance. "If you weren't such a freaking nun, you'd know when a guy is bonkers in love with you. Spoiler alert: when he practically throws a rival through a window, that's your first clue."

"You heard about that?"

"Oh, honey, *everyone* heard about that."

My cheeks burned as I reached to pull the hood of my hoodie over my head. "Fantastic."

"After you left, the guys were all fired up for a fight, but of course no one had the balls to try and retaliate. The girls were all freaking out at how romantic the whole thing was. Seriously, best party ever." She gave me another glance. "Although I wouldn't expect to be welcome at the Alpha Theta Delta house again anytime soon."

I smirked. "I'll live."

"So you know I'm going to want all the details."

Before I could respond, we both spied Luka walking toward us. He was dressed in a pair of jeans and a black, long-sleeved thermal shirt with a heavy silver chain around his neck.

Brooklyn let out a low whistle. "Damn, he's fucking hot."

I gave her a playful shove.

She continued, "And an *older* man. Damn girl. Good for you. Why mess with the boys when you can have a real man."

Luka must have heard what she said because he smiled and gave her a wink. "Hello, Brooklyn."

She giggled. Actually giggled. "Nice to see you again."

Luka's voice was like dark honey. "Thanks again for your help at the party."

Brooklyn blushed. Jesus, she was blushing now? "Anytime."

My lips thinned. Were they flirting? Was she fucking

flirting with my man? Well, he wasn't my man, but he was... oh, fuck, I didn't know how I felt about Luka, but I did know I didn't like my friend eye-fucking him like he was her last meal.

I crossed my arms over my chest. "Is there something you want?"

Luka turned his heated gray gaze on me. He surveyed me from top to toe. My cheeks burned even brighter at the suggestive way his eyebrow rose.

Before he could respond with something so outrageously sexy both Brooklyn and I melted right into the sidewalk, I cut him off. "You know what I meant. I don't have time to talk. I'm headed to the darkroom."

Luka held out his arm. "And I'm your escort."

I hesitated, but not wanting to cause Brooklyn to be concerned or ask any more questions, I placed my hand in the crook of his arm. I called out over my shoulder as we turned toward the Arts & Culture building, "I'll call you later."

Brooklyn called back, "Don't worry if you're too *busy* to call."

I turned to Luka. "Seriously, what are you doing here?"

"I'm not allowed to want to spend time with you?"

"We spent the whole weekend together."

And what a fucking weekend it had been. We spent the entire time in his hotel suite. It was like a montage scene from some rom-com movie. Him feeding me strawberries. Bubble baths. Reading together. Lounging on the sofa. Lots of crazy sex—I certainly was making up for lost time in that regard. He even had a personal shopper drop off clothes for me. Which of course led to a mini-fashion show of what he bought, which then lead to a striptease show.

The whole thing was very boyfriend- and girlfriend-like.

It had been romantic and fun and sexy, which was why it could never ever happen again.

No Russians. It was my hard and fast rule, and I was going to stick to it.

"I have work to do on my photography project."

"I'm coming with you."

"You don't need—"

"I'm coming with you. End of argument."

I pulled open the heavy door to the Arts & Culture building and let it go the moment I passed, not caring if it hit him in the nose. I stomped down the stairs that led to the open basement level. Tossing my backpack and my blue camo purse on the table, I pulled out the negatives I wanted to work with. "Don't you have a job or something you need to get back to?"

Luka smiled. "Nope. You have my *complete and undivided* attention."

I sighed. Resigned to my fate of having him watch over me for the next few hours, I opened the door to my favorite darkroom and paused. Visions of the horrifying moments from the last time I was in this room flashed before my eyes. Closing it quickly, I moved several doors down and opened that one.

Luka frowned. "What was wrong with the last one?"

I averted my face. "Nothing."

Luka cursed under his breath. He followed close

behind me into the small darkroom. Just as I turned, he wrapped an arm around my waist and pulled me close.

He placed a finger under my chin and lifted my face up to his gaze. "You're safe with me. You know that, right?"

The very last thing in the world I am is safe with him.

He stroked my cheek. "I'm not going to let anyone harm you, ever again."

Uncomfortable with the fierceness of his sentiment, I teased, "What are you going to do? Follow me around for the rest of my life keeping all the baddies away?"

His eyes narrowed. "Yes, precisely that."

I tried to step back, but his arm tightened. "I was just kidding."

"I'm not."

"Luka, you can't follow me around as my personal bodyguard for the rest of our lives. *You* have a life to get back to. *I* have a life to get back to."

"I was thinking more husband than bodyguard."

I blinked several times. I must have heard him wrong. "What did you just say?"

"You heard me."

I shook my head. "I'm not marrying you, Luka."

"Why not?"

This time I did break away from him. "Why not? Because of a thousand reasons." I ticked them off on my fingers. "We only just met. Our age difference. The fact that I'm only twenty-two and have no plans of marrying anyone. You're Russian with ties to my horrible family."

"You are Russian too, Katia."

"It's Katie," I shouted.

Luka stormed forward, pinning me against the low

counter. He placed a hand on either side of my hips. "It's Katia. Your name is Ekaterina Egorovna Novikova. You have the same Russian blood as I, and I'm fucking tired of you denying it. Denying us."

My eyes narrowed. "I'm not marrying you."

Luka leaned down and kissed me hard on the lips. "You don't have a choice."

"What is that supposed to mean?"

Luka stepped back and ran a hand over his eyes. "Your father didn't hire me to rescue you from the yakuza. He hired me because he thought you learned he planned to marry you off to Pavel Petrov and had run off."

My eyes filled with tears. I swiped at them with the back of my hand, angry I had shed even a single tear for the bastard. I had always known my father never gave a damn about me and of course I had overheard his dastardly plans for me when Luka and Dimitri were talking after I was kidnapped. I didn't know why it should upset me to hear it confirmed by Luka himself. "Why Pavel Petrov?"

"He's the seventy-year-old head of the Petrov family. They are more powerful in Russia than here in America. He has two sons, both idiots, who are based more out of Chicago. Your father is getting a nice payment from him as I understand it."

No wonder my father liked the man. It sounded like our family. My half-brothers were also both idiots who got themselves rightfully killed for crossing the Ivanov family.

"So my father hired you to find me and drag me to Moscow to marry some corpse and you agreed to it?"

I wasn't the least bit surprised at the depths of evil my family was capable of for their own selfish needs. Why couldn't my father just accept I wanted nothing to do with him? He couldn't possibly have thought I would have played the dutiful daughter and agreed to an arranged marriage to a man I'd never met, who lived in Russia!

Yet somehow Luka's betrayal hurt more. It shouldn't, but it did. No wonder he continued to follow and stalk me after he had safely rescued me. I had allowed myself to forget that rescuing me had never been the plan. Bringing me back to Moscow for an arranged marriage was the plan. What he had been hired to do. He was probably only biding his time until I became complacent enough to agree to follow him to Russia. All of this was probably just a ruse to make me fall in love with him so I would agree to a *fun romantic trip*. One that ended with me married to a corpse.

"It's true. You were just a job. At first. That all changed, even before I met you. When I was tracking you down, I got ahold of some of your photographs. You are very talented. I guess I started to learn about you through your work."

"My photographs? You mean the ones on the camera I tossed when I was grabbed? You didn't see—" I thought of the naked images I had taken as an experiment in lighting and contrast.

The corner of his mouth lifted. "Those are some of my favorites."

My mouth dropped open. "Oh, my God! Those were private!"

"Trust me, I have no intention of sharing those images with anyone, nor will I allow you to share them."

I snorted. "Trust you. Trust you? Oh, that's rich! Trust the man who has been lying to me from the beginning."

Luka snatched me to him. He fisted my hair and pulled my head back. His gaze moved from my eyes to my mouth and back. "I never lied to you. I didn't tell you the whole truth because I was shielding you from the pain I knew your father's intentions would cause. Regardless of what did or did not happen between us, I never had any intention of taking you to Russia to marry another man."

Tears escaped the corners of my eyes. "I saw the plane tickets to Russia in your bag."

"Those were purchased by your father. You don't honestly think I'd travel to Russia in economy, do you?"

His attempt at levity was lost on me. I was too upset and confused. "You need to leave. I need time alone to think."

Luka breathed deeply through his nose. The telltale angry twitch appeared near his right eye. "I'm not going anywhere."

My lips thinned as I talked through clenched teeth. "Listen, your *job* is over. I'm no longer your responsibility. I'm not going with you to Russia. And I'm definitely not marrying... *anyone*."

I emphasized the *anyone* by shoving away from him.

Luka lunged.

He picked me up and spun, pressing me against the closed door. He pushed his hips into mine as he clasped my jaw in his hands. "You listen to me, princess. You belong to me now. I'll do everything in my power to protect you. *That includes marrying you.* It's the only way you will be safe from your family's schemes. So even if I have to tie and gag you to the goddamn altar, know this, you will be my wife."

Then he kissed me. His tongue pushed past my lips and took control. It wasn't a passionate kiss, but one of dominance. As he deepened the kiss, his hard cock pressed against my stomach. His fingers moved from my jaw to wrap around my neck, holding me in place.

I reached up to grip his arms. Once again, I felt myself tumbling helplessly in the wind, caught in his storm.

Luka reached for the zipper on my jeans. He unzipped them and yanked them down to my knees. He then turned me to face the door. His hands gripped my waist as he pulled my hips toward him. Over our heavy breathing I could hear him lower his own zipper.

The head of his cock brushed my entrance. With no further foreplay, he thrust in deep. My body surged forward. I braced myself against the door.

He thrust again. I was aroused, but not completely ready for his brutal pounding. Pain mixed with pleasure as my body struggled to accept his thick shaft.

He wrapped an arm around my shoulders and lifted me up, and as he continued to thrust in deep, he rasped into my ear, "You feel that, babygirl? You feel my cock deep inside of you?"

I couldn't respond.

He tightened his embrace as he growled, "Answer me."

"Yes! Yes, I feel you."

"That's the only fucking cock you'll ever feel in this

tight pussy. Do you understand me? You're mine and no one is separating me from you. Not even you."

"Please," I begged as I reached down to tease my clit as he continued to thrust into me.

"Beg me. Beg me to fuck you harder."

Without hesitation, I shamelessly begged him. "Oh, God, fuck me. Please, I'm so close."

He grabbed my hair and shifted our bodies. He bent me over the counter as he placed a restraining hand on my lower back. He then unleashed the beast. Pounding into me so hard and fast the breath was forced from my body. I clawed at the countertop as my orgasm built.

He slapped my ass. The painful, sharp sting sent me over the edge. I screamed my release. Moments later, Luka was right there with me. Filling me with his come as he slapped my ass several more times.

I leaned my forehead against the cool countertop as I struggled to catch my breath.

Luka pulled out. He then swept his fingers over my pussy. He fisted my hair and pulled me upright to lean against his body. He raised his arm and swept his fingertips over my open lips, smearing them with a mixture of his come and my arousal, branding me with the wicked taste of us.

"You're mine, Katia. And soon we will speak the words that will bind us together before God and man."

I closed my eyes. "Please don't do this, Luka."

Luka stepped back and zipped up his jeans. "It's done. And don't even think about running from me. I'll find you. *I'll always find you.*"

He stormed out of the darkroom.

Swallowing a sob, I bent over and pulled my jeans and panties back up. As the denim scraped my spanked skin, I let out a hiss.

I was trapped. If Luka had his way I would no longer be Katie, free-spirited photographer. I'd be Katia, Russian wife—I placed a hand over my flat stomach—and maybe even mother.

It was too much.

I sank to my knees and cried.

CHAPTER 23

*L*uka

"Still not speaking to me?"

Katia lifted her chin and turned her head to stare out the window, willfully ignoring me.

I had borrowed a Lexus LX black SUV from Gregor in order to transport Katia and all her camera equipment to Damien and Yelena's house. We were speeding along the Rock Creek Parkway heading to the Virginia suburbs of Washington, D.C. It was still very early morning. The plan was for her to capture the early morning sunlight for the shoot, and then get back to campus in time for her afternoon classes.

Despite her being angry with me over our argument yesterday, she was too intrigued to turn down a paying photography gig, especially not a fashion shoot for an up-and-coming designer like Yelena Ivanova.

It had been torture not having her in my arms last night, but I knew she needed time and space to get used to the idea of us marrying. I'd like to think that if the situation had been different, I would give her all the time she needed, weeks, months, maybe even years, but I was lying. The truth was that I loved her, and I had no intention of letting her spend another week, let alone an entire year, without the protection of my name. I wanted her to be mine in all things. I wanted my child in her belly. I wanted her in my bed. I wanted it all and I wasn't going to wait to get it. She would come around eventually. I would give her no other choice.

I turned off the main road onto a long, winding tree-lined private drive. Damien's house was on the outer edge of Gregor's compound. It was easier to keep everyone safe and protected if they lived close. Besides, their wives, along with Gregor's sister Nadia, were inseparable friends.

I glanced over at Katia's profile.

Maybe if she got along with Samara, Yelena, and Nadia, we could consider settling down here. Or maybe I could introduce her to Dimitri's and Vaska's wives in Chicago? I didn't give a damn where we lived as long as she was by my side. I knew better than to even consider bringing Katia home to Russia for now. I would have to wait till the furor over her marrying me instead of her father's choice died down first to be absolutely certain she was safe.

Finally she spoke. "I want you to know I'm still very angry with you, and I'm only doing this for my career, not you."

I hid my smile. "Duly noted."

"I haven't changed my mind about marrying you."

I nodded again. "Noted as well."

She huffed. "We're not getting married."

I stayed silent as I navigated a turn.

She turned in her seat to face me. "Luka. I need you to understand. I'm not marrying you. Ever. It's nothing personal. I've sworn never to marry a Russian or get involved in the slightest way with my family's business."

I still stayed silent.

She sighed. "I thought about this a lot last night. It just would never work between us. I don't want to be a wife. I want to have a career. I want to travel the world taking photographs."

I frowned. "What have I ever done or said that would give you the impression I didn't want those things for you as well?"

She mimicked a heavy Russian accent with a little Neanderthal mixed in for good measure. "You mine. We fuck now. I put baby in belly."

I lifted an eyebrow as I cast a sidelong glance in her direction. "Me Tarzan. You Jane."

She stuck her tongue out at me and turned her head back toward the window.

"Don't stick that tongue out unless you plan to use it."

She said nothing, but I saw her squirm and readjust her seat.

Damien stepped out of his front door to greet us as we arrived.

After hefting her camera bags on my shoulder, I placed

a hand at the small of her back and led her forward. "Katia, this is my friend Damien Ivanov."

She started to correct me, but I squeezed her waist and sent her a warning glance.

After a moment's hesitation, she said, "Nice to meet you."

"My wife, Yelena, is very excited to meet you. Follow me."

Instead of going into the house, we followed him around to the backyard. There was a large structure that looked like a Colonial barn house. It had white-washed wooden slats and black wrought-iron accents. Instead of the typical double doors on the upper floor that led to the haylofts, it had a stunning set of windows.

Damien gestured to the building. "Do you like it? We just finished converting it into a fashion studio."

We followed him into the building. The lower level was obviously used for storage. There were bolts upon bolts of stacked fabrics in all sorts of colors and textures as well as dress forms and mannequins of various sizes and several sewing machines.

Damien called up the staircase to the open loft above. "Yelena! Angel? Luka and Katia are here."

A blonde woman with large bright blue eyes leaned over the railing. "Yay! Come right up!"

The moment we reached the top of the stairs, Yelena grabbed Katia and hugged her in a warm embrace. "I'm so glad you're here! Thank you so much for offering to photograph my designs."

Katia looked a little taken aback by the warm show of affection. She stood there for a minute with her arms stiffly at her sides before she returned the hug. "You're welcome. Thank you for giving me the chance."

Yelena stepped back and clapped. "This is going to be so much fun!"

Katia surveyed the open loft. Every corner had either a sewing machine or a mannequin with an article of clothing on it. "I love all the light. Do you have models or are we just photographing the clothes? We could use the white clapboard walls as kind of a rustic background in contrast to the glamour of the clothes, or we could scope out another location on the property if you prefer."

Yelena laughed as she laid her head on Damien's shoulder. "She's totally a Capricorn."

Katia looked at me then back at Yelena. "What?"

Yelena waved off her concerns. "It's this thing I do. I like to guess people's zodiac sign. You are a total Capricorn. Am I right?"

Katia smiled. "Actually you are."

Yelena clapped again. "I knew it." She turned to me. "I can tell just by the way you're standing that you are a Virgo."

I nodded. "Right again."

Damien's eyes filled with pride as he looked at his beautiful wife. "She's rarely wrong."

Yelena's bright eyes widened with glee. She grabbed her phone and playfully held it up to Damien's mouth. "Can I get you to say that again for the recording?"

He kissed her forehead. "Hell, no."

I handed Katia her camera bags as Yelena pulled her to the other side of the studio. Damien gestured to a small lounge area. There were two large sofas and a coffee table that was covered with small plastic toys. Damien gestured to the toys. "She has this obsession with McDonald's Happy Meal toys. She says they are her good luck charms. Like a sucker I buy them for her whenever I get a chance."

I sat down and picked up one of the pink cartoon characters. A few months ago, I might have made fun of him for such a soft, sentimental gesture. Not today. Today I found myself hoping that one day Katia and I would share a similar silly romantic thing.

We sat back and watched the girls in silence. Enjoying seeing them collaborate.

Yelena rolled one mannequin close to the window. "I really want to capture the detail work on this one. I want close-ups of all the beading and lace."

Katia raised her camera and took a few shots. She checked the LED window and flipped through the shots, then nodded. She held the camera to the side for Yelena to see. "The lighting works. Although I think we should pivot it more toward the window to really capture the ivory glow of the lace in the sunlight."

Yelena nodded. "Love it." She then tucked her arm through Katia's and pulled her to the next mannequin. She gestured to a baby blue gown with a long flowing skirt. "So I think we should wait to photograph this one until the next time when I have models here. I just think this one needs the fluid movement of being on a body to really capture it. Otherwise it just looks flat."

"Wait!" Katia ran over to me and searched through her bags. "Darn it."

I leaned over. "What are you looking for? Is it in the car?"

She shook her head and sighed. "No. I wanted to show her this series I did with some ballet students, but I didn't bring the memory card."

I pulled out my phone and opened the photo files. I flipped through a few images. "You mean these?"

She took my phone from me and stared at the screen before looking back at me. "You have these on your phone? Why?"

I rose to stand over her. Turning my back to shield us from Damien and Yelena, I stroked her cheek. "They are on my phone because you took them. I haven't done a very good job of telling you how talented I think you are if you have to ask why. These photos are gorgeous. They belong on a museum wall."

She stared up at me. There was a spark of... something... behind her crystal blue eyes. Awareness? Maybe even love?

She seemed to shake the emotion off. She looked up at me with narrowed eyes. "Nice try. I'm still not marrying you."

As she tried to stalk away, I swung out my arm and smacked her on her cute ass. She threw me an angry look before taking my phone to show Yelena her photos.

I rejoined Damien on the sofa.

He looked over at me. "She doesn't know yet, does she."

I shook my head. "Nope."

"So when do you plan to tell her that three days from now at noon, she's going to become your blushing bride?"

I looked at my watch. "In two days, eight hours, and thirty-seven minutes."

Damien chuckled as he shook his head. "So it's going to be one of *those* kinds of weddings. No judgment here, my friend. For a while there, I thought Yelena would be saying her vows while chained to my wrist and possibly through a gag."

"How did you get her to finally say yes?"

Damien raised an eyebrow and waved a hand down his body. "Who would say no to this charming package?"

"Is it true she once threw a brick at you?"

Damien frowned. "A difference of opinion. She wanted to run, and I wanted her to stay."

At least I wasn't the only one with an unusual courtship.

I looked over at Katia. She was entirely in her element, chatting animatedly with Yelena as she snapped some trial photos. She was so beautiful and talented. It was no wonder I would sacrifice everything I had to keep her with me. If that woman asked for the world, I would give it to her no matter the cost. Without taking my eyes off her, I said, "It's worth it in the end, though, right?"

Damien looked over at his wife. "Absolutely."

A staff member brought us some tea and pastries as we were content to talk business and watch as our women worked.

It was a pleasant morning—until Yelena brought out the wedding dress.

Katia exclaimed when she saw the champagne silk gown, "Oh, this is my favorite of your collection so far. It's beautiful. I love the ivory silk with the silver embroidery on the bodice."

Yelena laughed. "Well, I'm glad you like it. I mean, it's

your wedding gown after all. Which reminds me, we should squeeze in a quick fitting before you leave today, otherwise I'll never have enough time to make the alterations before Saturday."

Katia stilled.

I could feel the blood freeze in my veins as she slowly turned to look at me. Without taking her eyes off me, she said to Yelena, "Did you say *my wedding dress?*"

Unaware of Katia's change in mood, Yelena fluffed the full skirt. "Yes. I have three other ones in my collection, but Luka picked out this one for you yesterday. He said it was perfect and now that I've met you, I completely agree. Your man has good taste. And don't you worry about it being ready by Saturday. You have such an amazing body, I doubt I'll have to make many alterations. Perhaps just a little off the hem and maybe take it out slightly in the bust."

As Yelena chatted on, Katia never took her eyes off me.

Fuck.

CHAPTER 24

Luka

BEFORE SHE COULD UTTER another word, I stormed across the room and swept her up into my arms and over my shoulder.

Damien called out to my retreating back, "Through the back door. Third door on the right."

I raised an arm to show I heard him.

Katia pounded on my back as she let out a long stream of very creative curses. "You low-down, son-of-a-bitch bastard dirty swine asshole lying gorilla!"

I ducked low as I carried her out of the refurbished barn and across the lawn to the main house. I opened the back door and counted till I reached the third door. I kicked it open and surveyed the spacious spare bedroom before dropping Katia down on the king-size bed.

She immediately bounced up and climbed off it. Her

eyes narrowed. Her breathing was fast and heavy with anger. "I wouldn't marry you on Saturday if you were the last—"

I placed my hands on either side of her face, cradling her jaw in my palms. I walked forward, pushing her until her back hit the wall. Then my mouth descended, capturing hers.

The moment my tongue slipped past her lips, she bit it.

My head jerked back as I tasted copper.

My eyes narrowed. "You want to play rough, princess? Let's play rough."

I pierced my fingers into her hair at the base of her skull, closing them into a fist and pulling on her hair. My mouth descended a second time. This time I held her jaw open with my other hand. Pushing the tips of my fingers into her soft cheeks, preventing her from biting down. I wanted her to taste my blood on her tongue. I speared my tongue in and out of her mouth, thrusting and dueling with hers. I pushed my hips against her body, pinning her against the wall.

I swallowed her groan as her body began to melt into mine.

Wrapping an arm around her waist, I swung her around until we both were standing at the end of the bed. I tore off my T-shirt before tearing at the knot that kept her patterned wrap dress in place.

She placed her hands over mine. "Wait! No! We can't do this. We need to talk."

"After," I growled before loosening the knot and opening her dress to expose the pretty pink lace panty and bra set she was wearing.

I placed my hand around her waist and lifted her high before tossing her back onto the center of the bed.

I kicked off my boots as I reached for my belt.

Her eyes focused on the thick strap of leather as I pulled it free of my belt loops. I should punish her. Nothing would please me more than bending her over this bed and strapping her ass raw with my belt, but now was not the time.

I tossed the belt aside and pulled off my jeans. I joined her on the bed, naked.

I slowly pulled down her panties as I kept my gaze on hers. Kneeling between her open thighs, I ran a finger over her pussy. "Ask me to kiss your pussy."

She bit her lip.

Fuck, I loved how stubborn she was.

I raised my hand and slapped her between the legs.

Her hips rose off the bed as she cried out in pain.

"I said, ask me to kiss this pussy."

"Please kiss my pussy," she breathed.

I placed my hands under her ass and lifted her high. I wanted her to know who was in complete control of her body. I ran my tongue down and up the seam before pushing deep to tease her entrance. I feasted on her honeyed flesh, flicking her clit with the tip of my tongue until she moaned her release. The moment she did, I leaned over her and thrust in deep, wanting to capture the tremors and clench of her pussy as she came.

I settled my forearms on either side of her head. "Look at me, princess."

Her sapphire eyes locked on mine.

I thrust in slowly, wanting her to feel every inch as I claimed her.

She reached up to grab my shoulders.

I bit then licked her lower lip. "You're marrying me."

Katia arched her back as her legs wrapped around my waist, pulling me in deeper. "No, I'm not."

I thrust in harder. "Yes, you are."

I pulled her left nipple into my mouth. I swirled my tongue around the sensitive flesh before sucking it in deeper.

Katia moaned and clawed at my shoulders.

I ran my tongue up the smooth column of her neck before nipping at her earlobe. "You don't have a choice."

She ran her fingernails down my back as she rasped against my neck, "Fine. I'll let you be my boyfriend."

I groaned as I shifted my hips to press against her core. "Fuck being a boyfriend. I'm your *husband*." I punctuated the last word with a piercing thrust.

She leaned up to place a hard kiss on my mouth before sinking her teeth into my lower lip. She pulled on it hard before leaning back to stare at me with defiant crystal blue eyes. "Not unless I say yes."

I wrapped my arm around her and flipped our bodies until she was straddling me. I placed my hands on her hips, raising her slightly so her body could absorb the impact of mine. I lifted my hips to pound into her tight pussy hard and fast. Her beautiful breasts bounced with each thrust as her hair fell in loose wild waves over her shoulders and down her back.

She looked like a fucking goddess. And she was all mine.

I reached up to pinch her right nipple. "You say yes, every time I fuck you."

I slipped my hand between us to tease her clit. "You say yes, every time you come on my cock."

I cupped her ass cheeks and squeezed. "You say yes, every time your body accepts my seed."

Her eyes widened. She started to rise up on her knees to escape me.

I flipped our bodies again, covering her with mine, weighing her down into the thick covers.

She seethed. "Don't you dare do it, Luka. Not again."

My mouth hitched at the corner. I wrapped my hands around her slim thighs and lifted them high around my waist. I tilted my hips to make sure I was thrusting deep as well as brushing her sensitive nub. Her eyes glazed over as her mouth opened on a moan. Her fingernails dug into my shoulders as she came a second time. Her inner muscles squeezed my shaft. The dark pleasure sent me over the edge.

I pounded into her several more times as my cock swelled and my balls tightened. Reaching for her arms, I pinned them down to the bed, then laced my fingers through hers. I thrust one more time. Pressing in so deep my balls caressed the soft bottom curve of her ass.

Her eyes widened as she bucked her hips, but she couldn't dislodge me.

I released deep within her, filling her with my come.

"Damn you," she raged.

I pulled out slightly and thrust again, making sure her body absorbed every drop. "Say you'll marry me."

"Why are you doing this? Why marriage? Why can't we just date for a while?"

I raised an eyebrow. "Do I look like the kind of man who fucking dates?"

She scrunched her nose. "Not exactly."

I stayed inside her body as I leaned down. "I'm doing this to keep you safe. Until you marry, you will never be safe from your father's machinations."

"Can't we just say we married, but not really go through with it?"

"No."

She sighed. "Can we get married and then get an annulment or divorce as soon as things die down?"

"No."

"Why do you keep saying no? These are perfectly reasonable options."

I kissed her on the forehead. "Not when you could be carrying my baby they're not."

"If you stopped having unprotected sex with me, we wouldn't have to worry about that."

I smirked. "No."

It wasn't something I worried about. It was something I wanted. It wasn't enough to have her by my side. I wanted to see her arms cradling our child. I wanted a little girl with her gorgeous eyes or a little boy with her stubborn chin. For the first time in my life, I wanted to share my life with someone and only Katia would do.

"You're impossible! There's no way I'm pregnant and I'm going on birth control first chance I get."

"Try it and see what happens."

"You're a big bully, you know that?"

My cock started to harden again within her tight, warm body. "I'm aware. Does this mean you'll marry me, or do I have to tie you up and carry you to the altar?"

She turned her head to avoid my gaze. Her voice was low and hoarse when she asked, "Why would you sacrifice so much just to keep me safe?"

I turned her head to meet my gaze. "Because I want to wake up with you in my arms every morning." My shaft lengthened, fully engorged. I thrust slowly. "Because you challenge and enrage and enthrall me."

I kissed her lips as I continued to slowly push into her body. "Because I've begun to crave the sound of your laughter." I curled a hand under her right knee and lifted her leg high, angling my hips to push deeper into her body. "Because you are beautiful, talented, intelligent, and very entertaining to be around."

Her body arched under mine.

I thrust again. "Because I'm a man who has lived a thousand lives in thirty-three years and I don't need a month, a year, or even a week to know who I want to spend the rest of my life with and why."

I kissed the curve of her jaw, then her lips. "Because I want to be there when you succeed, and I want to kiss your tears and make it all better when you fail. Because I want to see you hold our child in your arms as you gaze up at me. Because I'm tired of walking this cold Earth alone. I need your warmth, Katia."

She reached up to circle her arms around my neck. "Luka…" she breathed.

I increased the pace of my thrusts. "Because I love you, babygirl."

CHAPTER 25

Katie

THE LAST TIME someone told me they loved me was my mother right before she died. It was easy enough to live without hearing those words. You just went about your day. You ate, slept, went to class, had fun with friends. You functioned. You got by. You lived your life.

And then someone tells you they love you.

And everything changes.

With those three simple words, the life you were leading previously seemed cold and empty. Things were different because somewhere out in that brutal, unfeeling, harsh world... someone loved you. Someone cared about what happened to you. Someone wanted to see you happy and safe. Suddenly, you *mattered* to someone.

I wouldn't insult Luka by accusing him of lying, of saying anything to get me to agree to marry him. I wouldn't insult him like that. I hadn't known him for long, but I've known him long enough to know he had plenty of ways to force me to the altar without telling me he loved me. If he said it, he meant it.

I wasn't sure what was crazier.

The fact that he loved me... or the fact that I might actually love him too.

No one would argue that he was a hard man to love. He was arrogant, pushy, stubborn, and practically a Neanderthal in the bedroom. But he was also funny, sweet, intelligent and... well... *practically a Neanderthal in the bedroom.*

I couldn't get the image of him lounging on the sofa wearing a pair of cute reading glasses while he read Hemingway and commented on the different subjects from my homework out of my head. Something told me that unguarded moment was the real Luka, not the bloodthirsty man who barged into the frat house and almost threw a boy through a window for touching me. From the moment we met, I'd never given him a chance. I'd painted him with the Russian criminal brush and moved on. Yet time and time again, he had shown me he was more than what he seemed.

Despite all this, I couldn't say *I love you* back to him.

His eyes gleamed bright silver as he stared down at me. His weight pressed me deeper into the soft mattress; I could still feel his cock inside of me. The intimacy of the physical connection made his words that much more intense.

I averted my gaze, turning my head to the side.

Luka caressed my jaw and turned my head back to

face him. "Don't look so worried, princess. I don't expect you to say anything back."

"I just need time."

He frowned as he ran his thumb over my bottom lip. "Baby, I would move mountains to give you anything in the world you asked for... except time."

"This isn't fair. Two weeks ago I was an American college student worried about an art history paper I had due and now I have two unwanted fiancés, one a Russian corpse and the other a Russian criminal!"

"That is where you are wrong. You were never an American college student. You are and have always been the daughter of a powerful Russian family. You must have known this day would come?"

I gripped his shoulders. "Can't you just let me leave? I'll disappear. I promise this time my father will never find me."

"No. You will never be safe. Your only protection is to remain by my side."

"Anonymity would be my protection."

Luka pulled out and rolled off me. He adjusted his jeans over his hips and zipped them up. He lifted up his leather belt. My heart stopped. After pausing, he threaded the belt through his belt loops. "The answer is no. I will not argue over this, Katia. We marry on Saturday."

Clenching my jaw, I crawled off the bed and reached for my wrap dress. I shoved my arms into the sleeves and wrapped the dress tightly around my torso before knotting the belt. "We'll see about that," I muttered under my breath.

Luka crossed the room in a flash. He spun me about

and slammed me against the wall. Caging me in with his forearms, his lips thinned as he stared down at me. "Enough, Katia. Stop acting like a petulant child. Life is not fair. I am doing this to protect you and I will not have you doing anything reckless. Or so help me God, you will say your wedding vows tied naked to this bed, do you understand me?"

"You're nothing but a big bully, you know that?"

He kissed my forehead. "You'll get used to it."

Thankfully the hallway was empty when we finally exited the bedroom. I would have been mortified to have to face Yelena after the display Luka and I just put on. There wasn't a doubt in my mind both she and Damien knew precisely what we had been doing in their guest room.

Luka placed a hand at my lower back and escorted me through the house and out the front entrance. I was pleased to see all my camera equipment had been discreetly placed in the back seat of Luka's car. Luka held the passenger door open for me. As I sat, he reached over and buckled me in.

I sighed. "I'm perfectly capable of buckling my own seat belt."

Luka winked. "But then I would miss out on touching your amazing breasts." He pressed the back of his wrist against the curve of my left breast as he finished buckling the seat belt.

I clenched my inner thighs. What the hell? A week ago I was a virgin, not the least bit concerned with what I might be missing out on when it came to sex, and now I was a raging nympho who was ready to go again after just being fucked sideways not fifteen minutes ago.

Luka got behind the wheel and we made our way back down the winding driveway. Dusk was already falling. We turned out of Damien's property and onto a country highway, the thick overhang of trees making it seem even darker than it was.

Several miles down the road, the first black SUV came out of nowhere. It burst through the tree line from some small dirt lane, blocking the road directly in front of us.

Luka called out, "Fuck!"

He slammed on the brakes and threw the car into reverse. "Get down!" The car swerved as he swung it around and raced forward in the opposite direction.

I tried to lower my torso but was jerked back by the seat belt strap. My hands were shaking as I reached to unbuckle it. I tried several times, but I couldn't press the button. My hands were shaking too badly. Luka's strong hand covered mine. I met his stern gaze.

He nodded. "Don't worry, baby. I'll get you out of here."

He pressed the button with his thumb. The seat belt released so violently the metal portion slammed against the window.

Luka placed his hand on the back of my head and pushed me down until I was lying on his lap. My body rocked back and forth as the car swerved and picked up speed. Several gunshots rang out. The windshield splintered and cracked, obscuring the view.

"Cover your ears, babygirl."

Luka raised his Glock and fired through the windshield, shattering it further. It was now an opaque mosaic of cracked glass.

I swiveled back onto my seat and raised my legs into the air. With all my might, I shoved my feet against the windshield. It broke away like some kind of broken glass blanket, bouncing off the hood of our car and falling to the road.

Luka turned and winked at me before focusing his attention back on the road. A second black SUV blocked our escape. He kept one hand on the wheel as he raised his Glock a second time.

I knew he wouldn't be able to defensively drive and fire at the same time.

"Give it to me!" I shouted as I reached for the gun. I had never fired a gun before, but I was pretty sure I knew how.

Luka handed it over as he placed both hands on the wheel. "Get ready! On my mark!"

The SUV ahead was perpendicular to our car, completely blocking the road. On one side was a deep ditch filled with dirt, grass, and rocks. On the other was a small stream.

I racked the gun like Luka told me to and lifted it with both hands. My heart was beating so fast I could hear it over the roar of our car engine.

Luka raced toward the blockading SUV. At the last minute he turned the wheel, sending our car careening to the side. For a few brief seconds we were lined up parallel to the SUV. I could see the driver's shocked face through the driver's window.

"Now!" Luka shouted.

I straightened my elbows and pulled the trigger. The driver's side window shattered in a burst of glass. I could see the two occupants duck low to avoid the bullet spray. Hot brass bullet casings burned the tops of my thighs as I kept firing until I had emptied the magazine.

"I need more ammo!" I called out.

Luka turned the wheel again and headed back in our original direction. "Glove box."

I reached into the glove box for the only spare magazine. Luka snatched the gun from my hand, released the empty magazine, and clipped the new one into place before handing it back to me.

My body was tense as we barreled toward the next vehicle blocking our path.

Luka glanced in my direction. "Ready, baby?"

I nodded as I raised the gun and pointed it through the now-open windshield space. "Let's do this."

Luka smirked as he gripped the wheel harder. "Don't tell me you're not a Russian."

My tension eased as I heard the pride in his voice.

As we neared the first SUV, both the side windows rolled down. The long barrels of two AK-47s leaned out.

"Fuck!" raged Luka.

He grabbed my hair and forced me down just as the first spray of bullets hit our car. Blood splatter hit my cheek. I turned my head to see a sickening crimson stain blossom over Luka's right shoulder.

"You're hit!"

"Hold on, baby."

He turned the wheel again. The car lurched and tipped downward. The front end smashed against the rocks along the side of the stream before righting itself. Cool water splashed over the hood and hit us in the face as Luka took the car into the ditch and drove it through the stream.

Both of the black SUVs drove alongside, firing at us from above. There was a terrible popping noise as they hit their mark. Smoke rose from the open bullet holes in the hood. At the first barest opening in the trees to my right, Luka swerved. I bounced around in my seat as he pitched the car left then right, avoiding trees and boulders, driving us as deep as he could into the thick woods until the overgrowth became too much.

Luka took the gun from me. "Run, baby. Run as fast as you can and don't stop. I'll hold them off."

Tears sprang to my eyes. "I'm not leaving you!"

He placed his hand around the back of my neck and pulled me in for a hard, quick kiss. "I love you. Now do as I say and run!"

The blood had now soaked the entire front of his shirt.

I realized now he knew we wouldn't be able to outmaneuver our assailants, so he had driven into the woods to give me a fighting chance to get away. My running might be our only chance to get help. We couldn't be more than a few miles away from Damien and Yelena's place.

The two SUVS crashed through the trees toward us.

His silver eyes implored me. "Baby, you have to run. Please!"

"I'm going to get help." I opened the door and after glancing back at Luka one more time, I took off into the woods.

A bullet splintered a tree right over my head, sending

chips of wood showering down onto me. I ducked low and kept running. Gunfire shattered the silence of the coming evening as Luka desperately tried to cover my escape.

I hazarded a glance over my shoulder. Luka was standing on the hood of our SUV, firing down at the men as they approached, using the rest of the car as a shield. One of the men raised his gun and fired. I watched in horror as Luka's body absorbed the impact of the bullet and staggered back. He tumbled off the hood of the car and rolled several feet away.

He laid there, face down. Motionless.

"Luka!" I screamed.

Without any thought for my own safety, I ran back. I fell to my knees in the dirt and rolled him over. His eyes were closed. I couldn't tell if he was still breathing. His shirt front was covered in blood. I cradled his head in my lap as I wrapped my arms around his shoulders. I rocked back and forth. "Luka! Please! No!"

Hands snatched at my arms, dragging me away.

I kicked and screamed, screeching at the top of my lungs, "Murderers! You fucking assholes! Get off me!" I was like a madwoman, scratching and clawing, desperate to get back to Luka.

The last thing I saw was a fist coming for my face.

Then everything went black.

CHAPTER 26

Luka

I couldn't move my arms.

My body gently rocked back and forth as I tried to move my legs. Nothing.

Opening one eye, I looked down to see I was strapped to a gurney.

The muted sound of an ambulance siren registered in my pain-fogged mind.

I clenched my fists as I tried to raise my torso.

Hands pushed down on my shoulders. "Sir, don't move. You're in an ambulance. You've been shot. We're taking you to Saint Anne's hospital."

I tried to rise up again. "The fuck you are. Unstrap me."

The voice of the paramedic became insistent as a heart

monitor began to beep erratically. "Sir, please! You must lie down."

The driver of the ambulance called out, "What the fuck?"

The other paramedic in the back answered, "What's the matter?"

"There's an SUV blocking the road."

The ambulance siren blasted several times. The driver then said, "The idiot's not moving." Then his voice came over a loudspeaker. "Move your vehicle. This is an emergency."

I struggled to rise again. Fresh blood trickled from my chest wound, soaking the white gauze bandage.

The paramedic leaned over me, applying pressure. "Get us out of here. This guy's losing it. I'm not going to be able to keep him immobile much longer."

"I'm trying," called back the driver.

Just then there was a hard banging knock on the ambulance back doors right before they swung open. I leaned up to see Damien standing near the back bumper. "Did someone call an Uber driver?"

I fell back laughing.

The paramedic called out, "Hey! You can't be in here!"

Mikhail Volkov, head of security for the Ivanov family and brother-in-law to Damien and Gregor, appeared. "We're going to take it from here." He pulled out a thick roll of cash and sectioned off several hundred-dollar bills. He tossed them onto the seat next to the paramedic.

Damien jumped into the back cab of the ambulance and unbuckled my restraints. "Jesus Christ, Luka. You're not human. Do you have any idea how long we've been looking for your ass? We found your bullet-ridden car twenty minutes ago over a mile down the road. The cops were already on scene, but we took care of it. We heard over their dispatch radio about an ambulance call and figured it must be you."

I didn't respond. I wasn't entirely sure how I made it this far away from the scene of attack with my bullet wounds. All I knew was my one driving need was to rescue Katia.

Before we could discuss the matter further, the ambulance driver appeared near the back to confront Damien. "You can't take our patient. He's been shot. He needs to see a doctor."

Damien placed a hand on his shoulder. "We take care of our own. Take the money and get out of here. If you know what's good for you, this never happened."

The driver frowned and continued to argue. "But—"

Damien thrust a pile of cash into his hand. "Take the money, my friend. Trust me. You don't want this to get ugly."

I swung my legs over the side of the gurney and used Mikhail's arm for support as I stood up. Dipping down to avoid the low ceiling of the ambulance cab, I stepped toward the exit doors. Damien held out his arm and helped me step down. My knees almost buckled from the pain and loss of blood.

Mikhail hopped out of the ambulance. He snatched up the paramedics' go bag and shoved some additional supplies and medicine into it. "We're taking this too."

The paramedic stepped forward. "A thousand dollars."

Mikhail smiled as he tossed the additional cash into the ambulance. "I like you."

With the support of both Damien and Mikhail we made our way to their waiting SUV. "Is Katia with you?"

They exchanged a glance but didn't answer.

I repeated, "Dammit, is Katia with you? Is she safe?"

They refused to answer. I shrugged off their help and turned to head back in the opposite direction. "She's hiding in the woods. We have to find her."

Damien stepped in front of me. "She's not in the woods. I'm sorry, Luka. We were too late. They grabbed her."

I stumbled and would have fallen had Mikhail not grabbed my arm in time. My beautiful babygirl was in danger. I hadn't kept her safe. This had happened on my watch. She was my responsibility and I had failed her. The crushing sense of loss and rage was worse than the pain from the bullet in my shoulder and side.

"Who?" I asked through clenched teeth.

Damien answered. "Gregor is ready to brief us when we get back, but from what we can tell, it was her father with the help of the Petrovs."

Bile rose in the back of my throat as my vision blurred. "I'll kill them all."

Damien and Mikhail moved to grab my arms. "First, we need to patch you up… then we kill them all."

The three of us stumbled several times as they struggled to get me into the back of their SUV. Soon we were racing back to Damien's house.

Yelena met us at the door. "My God!"

Damien gave her a reassuring wink. "Don't worry,

angel. It would take more than a few pussy bullets to kill this bastard."

They carried me into the kitchen and laid me out on the table. Damien used scissors to cut away my shirt as Mikhail dumped the contents of the paramedics' bag onto the kitchen counter next to their own medical supplies. Bullet wounds were an unfortunate consequence of our business and none of us were fans of hospitals, so we were usually prepared. Mikhail was the one with the most battlefield hospital experience, so he was our default surgeon under such circumstances.

Mikhail approached with a syringe filled with what I knew to be propofol.

I shook my head. "No anesthesia."

"This isn't only a simple bullet graze, my friend. I'm not worried about your side, but I will have to dig the bullet out of your shoulder. It's going to hurt like a motherfucker."

I leaned back. "Do it. No drugs."

I deserved the pain. Katia was scared and in danger because of me. I didn't deserve sweet unconsciousness. I needed my mind to remain lucid and clear. The very moment Mikhail stitched me up I was going after the men who took her. I would get her back, and then I was never going to let her go.

Damien spoke to Yelena. "Go upstairs and grab every belt you can find." He turned back to me. "We'll have to strap you down. We can't risk you moving during the surgery."

I nodded.

Yelena returned. The men wrapped the belts around

my wrists and ankles and used the heavy wooden legs of the kitchen table which was held down by my own weight to secure me.

Yelena lifted my head and placed a bottle of vodka to my lips. "Drink this at least."

I chugged several gulps, letting the fiery liquid run down my chin.

Gregor walked in just as Mikhail was about to begin.

He leaned over my supine form. "She's alive."

I closed my eyes as relief swept over me. Thank God for that at least.

Gregor continued. "She's being held not too far from here somewhere in D.C. We just don't know the exact location yet."

"How do you know for sure?"

Gregor smiled. "Dimitri, Vaska, and Maxim paid a little visit to the Petrov brothers in Chicago. They beat the information out of them right before they put a bullet in their damn fool heads. Before the night is over, the Novikoffs and the Petrovs will know never to fuck with us again."

Mikhail's brow furrowed. "They should have learned that lesson after what they did to Nadia. We should have tracked that old bastard Egor down in Moscow and taken care of him then."

Gregor nodded. "I regret believing that old bastard had nothing to do with his sons' actions. We won't make that mistake again."

I nodded my head toward Mikhail. "Hurry up and get this bullet out of me so I can go get my girl."

They exchanged looks.

Damien spoke up. "We've got this. You've lost a lot of blood."

"Fuck you," I growled. "Katia is my responsibility. I'm not going to lay here while she's in danger. Now get this fucking bullet out of me or unstrap me so I can leave."

Gregor turned to leave. "I'm going to go check with our men. They're tracking down all leads to where they are keeping her."

Damien pulled a chair up to the table and rested his arm on its flat surface next to mine. He then rolled up his sleeve as he stuck a needle into the vein at his elbow. "We're about to become blood brothers."

He ran a tube to a needle in my own arm just as Mikhail leaned over me. "Brace yourself."

The pain was unbearable. Only the thought of Katia kept me from passing out. She needed me and I wasn't going to let her down again.

It took twenty agonizing minutes for Mikhail to dig out the bullet and any fragments left behind. Blood poured from my shoulder to drip down onto the tile floor. Sweat coated my brow and chest as I internalized all the pain. A ragged breath escaped my lips as I felt the prick of the needle, knowing it meant Mikhail was finally sewing me up.

"This won't be pretty."

"Don't care."

Damien tried to lighten the mood. "He'll have his rugged good looks to fall back on."

Mikhail wiped the blood off his hands and moved to inspect my side.

I tried to rise but the restraints prevented it. "Leave it for later."

Mikhail placed a restraining hand on my shoulder. "We need to stitch it up now, so it doesn't become infected and ruin all my good work. Besides, we don't have a location yet. Let's work on you until we know where to strike to rescue Katia."

He had a point. I gestured toward the bottle of vodka. Yelena lifted it to my lips again.

I would need my full strength if I was going to rampage against those who took Katia.

Mikhail got to work sewing up my side.

They finally unstrapped me when they finished. I rose up to a sitting position. I had to fight back a wave of nausea as my head swam. Someone handed me two pain pills. I popped them into my mouth and lifted the vodka bottle. I swallowed the pills with a swig of vodka.

Yelena returned to the kitchen with a gray thermal shirt and a pair of jeans. "These should fit."

I shrugged into the shirt. The moment I reached for the zipper to my jeans Damien covered her eyes and told her to leave. "Don't be corrupting my girl."

I smirked as I dropped my pants and pulled on the clean pair of jeans, wincing as the stitches in my shoulder pulled. "Do we have an update?"

At that moment Gregor strolled in. "Lock and load, boys. We have a location."

CHAPTER 27

Katie

I OPENED my eyes but could only see black.

I closed my eyes, wanting to sink deeper into that dark oblivion.

Luka was dead.

No. He couldn't be. Despite seeing the blood myself I couldn't fathom him dead. He was just too big and strong and full of life. He was a Russian gorilla of a man. Almost superhuman. A mere bullet couldn't possibly take down a man like Luka. Right?

A lump formed in the back of my throat as my chest tightened.

What if he was dead?

Oh, God, it would be all my fault.

I had killed the first and only man to ever show an interest in my welfare. The first man who ever said he loved me. The man who risked his own life to save me and had done nothing since but try to protect me from just this freaking scenario. Why hadn't I listened to him? Why had I assumed I knew better? He kept trying to warn me that the danger hadn't passed, and I stubbornly wouldn't listen.

He couldn't be dead.

He just couldn't be.

Not my Luka.

I couldn't imagine not seeing him smile again. Or that sexy way he would wink at me. Or the way he would call me his princess. Or how it felt to be held in his strong arms.

He's not dead.

He's not fucking dead.

I inhaled deeply. I needed to pull my shit together. Luka would expect me to keep a clear head until he was able to rescue me. I'd been through this bullshit before and survived. I would again. If not for myself, then for Luka.

I blinked several times. As my eyesight adjusted, I could see tiny flickers of light through a black cloth. They must have placed a hood over my head. The cowardly bastards. Knowing better than to move and alert them to the fact I was awake, I stayed still and listened, hoping for clues as to who had taken me and where I was.

By the soft cushion I felt under my shoulder, I could tell I wasn't in a car trunk. More like the back seat of a car.

Two men began to talk.

"*Oni zhdut v tserkvi.*"

"On budet v yarosti, chto my strelyali v neye pulyami."

Fuck. Why hadn't I kept up with my Russian? I could only pick up bits and pieces of their conversation. Someone was waiting for us at the church. The church? I thought I picked up the words *furious* and *bullets*. Maybe someone was going to be mad they'd fired on Luka and me?

"Zachem zlit'sya? Yego dragotsennaya, izbalovannaya suchka yeshcho zhiva, net?"

"Ty mozhesh' ob"yasnit' stariku, kak my poteryali dvoikh muzhchin i odnu iz yego mashin."

Well, I definitely knew that term. Precious spoiled bitch. My brothers and father had called me that enough times when I was a little girl to have that phrase seared into my brain. They also mentioned an old man.

Church.

Precious spoiled bitch.

Old man.

God dammit. My father was behind this. Of that I was certain. What the hell was his plan?

"My uzhe opazdyvayem. My mogli by ostanovit'sya i po ocheredi yebat etoo suchkoo."

Takes turns.

Bitch.

The blood in my veins froze. I didn't need to understand the whole sentence to know what they were discussing.

"A yesli starik uznayet?"

"My mozhem obvinit' v etom Luka. Skazhi stariku, chto on pohitil ego doch' i isnasiloval yeye."

They mentioned Luka and the word for daughter and rape. Were they planning on raping me and blaming Luka? Did that mean he was dead? They wouldn't be trying to frame him if he were still alive.

There was a long pause as I anxiously waited on the other man's response. I could hear them shifting in the front seat as if they were turning to stare at my inert body.

I waited, holding my breath, keeping as still as possible so as not to give away the fact that I was now awake.

Finally the man responded. *"Net. Ona slishkom khudaya. Krome togo, mne nravyatsya zhenshchiny, v kotorykh yeshcho yest' nemnogo zhizni."*

I had to stop my body from trembling in relief. He said no. It wasn't worth pissing off their boss, especially since they had to explain the loss of two of their men and one of the SUVs.

I didn't know how much time I had before we arrived at the church, but at least I knew they weren't going to pull the car over and take turns with me. It was a small comfort. I was still stuck in the back of a car with two armed assailants.

Carefully, hoping they didn't notice, I shifted my feet. I couldn't feel anything around my ankles, but it was better to be certain. I spread them apart a few inches; nothing restrained them. I already knew my hands weren't restrained so they were just banking on me staying unconscious.

I held my breath as the car rolled to a stop. After several seconds it continued on.

Tuning out their inane conversation about what they wanted to eat for lunch after dropping me off, I listened for any sounds outside the vehicle. There was no point in jumping out of the car if we were still in the countryside of Virginia, on the fringes of D.C. They'd recapture me quickly enough. They also might change their minds about raping me for their trouble.

It was better to take my chances and wait until I heard sounds of the city. At least assuming they were taking me in that direction. I desperately wanted to rip the hood off my head and peek out the window but stopped myself. Above all else, I needed to stay alive. I had to have hope that Luka had survived and would soon be on the hunt looking for me.

After another hour, I began to hear telltale signs of civilization. The honking of a horn. Traffic. The blare of a nearby car radio.

This time when the car came to a stop, I made a run for it.

I lurched upright and yanked the hood off my head. I pulled on the car door handle.

It was locked.

The men shouted out in alarm.

I flicked open the lock and pulled on the handle again.

As the door swung open, I propelled my body forward.

At that same moment, the man on the passenger side dropped his seat back. It hit me in the shoulder and pinned me to the back seat. Before I could squirm out from under it, he jumped out of the car and slammed my door shut. The car moved forward before he had even fully gotten back into his seat. The moment he did, he crawled into the back with me.

"Get the fuck away from me!" I shouted as I tried to head-butt him.

I raised my fists and clipped him on the jaw. Before I could hit him again, he snatched my wrists and held them tight.

"I guess I didn't hit you hard enough the first time."

I spit in his face. "Fuck you."

He transferred my wrists to one hand and slapped me so hard I fell back and slammed my head against the car window.

The man driving cried out, "Watch it, Nikolay! The boss will kill us if we return her with a beat-up face."

The asshole named Nikolay fired something back in Russian I didn't quite catch before reaching into his back pocket for a white zip tie. I fought him off as best as I could but, in the end, he tightly secured my wrists. He then placed the hood back over my head and secured it with a zip tie around my throat. It was so tight I had to take shallow breaths.

His foul breath could be smelled through the fabric of the hood as he leaned in close. "I'm going to enjoy fucking you the moment your new husband hands you over to his men."

Tears filled my eyes. I refused to give him the satisfaction of knowing how badly he terrified me with that statement.

I closed my eyes and felt the tears trickle over my cheeks.

Please please please be alive, Luka.

I need you.

I had no choice but to stay still and upright for the remainder of the ride. My lungs hurt from taking shallow breaths through the fabric. Finally the car came to a stop. Nikolay dragged me out of the car by my upper arm. I stumbled and fell to my knees on what felt like hard concrete. He yanked me upright and pushed me forward.

I could no longer see any light through the hood and judging by the echoes of our footsteps we were inside some building. I had no choice but to allow myself to be dragged along. In the distance, I could hear the low murmuring tones of conversation from a group of men. They stopped as we got closer.

I could hear someone ask in Russian why my hands were tied.

They then teased Nikolay and his partner for not being able to control one feeble girl.

My arms were roughly pulled forward. The cold edge of a knife blade brushed the sensitive skin of my inner wrist before the tight plastic band of the zip tie released. My hands immediately went to the zip tie around my throat, pulling it as far away from my skin as I could.

Nikolay leaned in close, his fetid breath choking me as he whispered, "Stay still. I'd hate to accidentally slit your throat."

The knife blade brushed the back of my hand before the zip tie fell away. I immediately dragged the hood off my head.

We were in an Orthodox Russian cathedral. The unsmiling faces of countless somber saints stared down at me from gilded frames. The spicy scent of incense choked the air. Everywhere I looked I saw the golden splendor of my youth. Memories of kneeling next to my mother, Sunday after Sunday, praying for the hitting and the abuse to stop rushed over me. All those unanswered prayers.

Finally, I leveled my gaze on the man who stood before me.

"Hello, daughter. Welcome to your wedding day."

CHAPTER 28

Katia

"You bastard! You killed him!"

I launched myself at my father. Throwing my full weight at him, we both tumbled to the marble-tiled floor. I straddled him and clawed my nails down his cheeks before pummeling his chest and face.

"Get her off me!" he screeched.

I scratched him again. This time catching the corner of his eye.

Hands scrambled to grab my arms, but I threw them off as I continued to rage against my father.

It took three men to pull me off him.

Several other men hastened to help him up off the floor. After he was finally standing, he angrily swatted them away. He stepped forward and raised his arm. I braced for the impact of his strike.

"You're not thinking of hitting my bride, are you, Egor?"

All eyes shifted to the man who entered the church from a side door behind the altar. He was pale and thin with only wisps of white hair on his mostly bald head. He leaned heavily on a cane as he shuffled forward. The shoulders of his suit were covered in white dander and there was a strange cream-colored stain on his tie.

I grimaced in revulsion as he approached.

Egor held a white handkerchief to his bleeding cheek and eye as he smirked in my direction. "Meet your future husband, daughter."

The man tried to bow but stumbled. The two men at his side grabbed his arms and righted him. "Pavel Maksimovich Petrov at your service." He then turned to Egor. "She looks strong with good hips. She will give me more sons."

Bile rose in the back of my throat. "I wouldn't marry you if you were the last person on Earth and you can't fucking make me."

Pavel turned to Egor, a frown on his face. "Egor, I paid you for a willing bride. I will not stand for this insubordination."

I let out a disgusted huff. "Paid for? You actually sold me like I was some piece of property you owned? My mother was right. You are nothing but a worthless piece of shit for a human being."

This time my father did hit me, striking me hard across the face. Foam formed at the corner of his mouth as he raged, "Shut the fuck up, bitch. You will do as you are told."

We all began shouting at once.

"I'm not marrying him!"

"Egor, control your daughter."

"You will obey me."

"Fuck you!"

"Watch your mouth!"

"I'm losing patience."

Egor turned to one of his men. "Bring the girl in."

Now I was torn. What did he mean by bring the girl in? Was he going to force some other poor woman to marry this decrepit corpse? This was awful. I wouldn't be able to live with myself if I saved my own skin at the expense of another woman. There had to be a way out of this.

I looked around the darkened church, but all the exits and entrances seemed to be guarded by my father's or Pavel's men. I was trapped.

There was a scuffle at the back of the church. I tried to turn and look but my father's men closed ranks behind me, standing shoulder to shoulder, blocking my view.

I could only helplessly stand there and listen to the clear sound of someone being dragged closer.

When they came into view, I gave a cry of alarm and surged forward. The men behind me held me back.

Brooklyn stood before me.

Her eyes were red-rimmed and wide with fear. There was a thick piece of duct tape over her mouth. Her usually bright hair hung limp and dull, with strands sticking to her tearstained cheeks. Her blouse was torn, and her jeans were filthy.

"Oh, my God! Brooklyn, I'm so sorry!" I turned on my

father. "She has nothing to do with this. She doesn't even know who I really am. Let her go!"

Egor nodded to one of his men. He forced Brooklyn to her knees. She started to scream and cry out through her gag. Once again, I tried to reach her, but was held back. "Brooklyn! Brooklyn!"

The man behind her raised a gun to her head. He ruthlessly pressed the barrel against her temple.

Fresh tears streamed down her cheeks.

I fell to my knees as well. "Stop! Don't hurt her!"

My father grabbed me by my hair and wrenched my head back. "Will you do as you are told?"

I nodded, refusing to take my eyes off my terrified friend.

He pulled on my hair, wrenching my neck again. "Answer me."

"Yes! Yes, I'll do whatever you want, just let her go."

Egor nodded again.

His man put his gun away and pulled Brooklyn to her feet.

Egor sneered at me. "After the ceremony."

I glared. "How do I know you'll let her go if I marry Petrov?"

He patted me on the cheek. "You're just going to have to trust your loving father, daughter."

He spat out the word like a curse, which was probably what it felt like. I remembered all those nights curled up in my bed, hearing him shout at my mother, praying she would just kill him. Now I truly wished she had. Years later, after she divorced him but still couldn't get free of his heinous clutches, she'd lamented that she hadn't driven a knife into his heart as he slept next to her. I vowed in this moment to see my dead mother's wishes through. The very first chance I got I was going to kill my father for all the hurt and harm he had caused me, my mother, Luka, and my friend.

Egor's man dragged Brooklyn back toward a side door.

"Brooklyn! No! I want her here with me."

"You will see your friend again when you are standing at the altar like an obedient daughter. Now go and get changed into your wedding dress."

I was dragged away in the opposite direction of Brooklyn. Guilt sat on my chest like a crushing weight. This was all my fault. If I had just been honest with her and told her what was going on in my life, she could have been more careful and protected herself. I foolishly thought I was protecting her by lying about my family and true name, but I had only put her directly in harm's way. I didn't believe for a second that my father would honor his word and let her go if I married Pavel. But I had no other choice except to move forward with this disgusting wedding and hope against hope that Luka was alive and would come in time to save us both.

I was shoved over the threshold into a small antechamber. It was obviously meant to be used as a makeshift bridal dressing room. There was a screen and a floor-length mirror. Resting on a nearby sofa was a white and gold wedding gown in a clear garment bag. Next to it was a pair of shoes and a garishly ornate wedding crown.

One of the men looked at his watch. "You have five minutes."

Refusing to look at him, I tossed over my shoulder, "Can I get some privacy, please?"

Both men adjusted their stances as they held their arms rigidly in front of them, each hand cupping the opposite wrist. "No," answered the closest one.

Knowing that every minute I wasted was another minute Brooklyn spent terrorized by my father's goons, I grabbed the dress and hastened over to the changing screen.

One of the men followed me. Shoving me out of the way, he kicked down the screen. "Don't pretend you need modesty. We know you were nothing more than Luka Siderov's whore."

A lump formed in the back of my throat. "Fiancée."

"What?"

I raised my chin. "I am Luka Siderov's fiancée and he is going to kill each and every one of you when he finds me."

They laughed. "Your fiancé was left face down in the dirt like a dog. He is dead."

I brushed at the tears forming in my eyes with the back of my hand. I refused to believe it. Luka would find me. If I believed anything about that man, it was that he would cheat death and move heaven and hell to find me.

Turning my back to them, I tore at the clear wrapping of the dress and pulled it off its wire hanger. Refusing to care, I stepped into it with my muddy shoes still on. The beads and gold threading scratched my skin as I pulled it up over my hips, under my wrap dress. I thought of the buttery soft silk of Yelena's wedding dress. I remembered with longing the elegant champagne color with simple lines and only a hint of embellishment around the bodice and how she said Luka had picked it out just for me. It had been perfect.

Yanking at the belt around my waist, I pulled the wrap dress off and the wedding dress up over my breasts, leaving my bra on. I bent my torso and stretched my arms to zip it up from behind. One of the men stepped forward to help but I scurried away. Eventually I got it zipped up. I glanced at my reflection in the mirror.

There were still smudged flecks of dried blood on my cheek. Luka's blood. I refused to wipe it off. My hair was a tangled mess with a twig wrapped around a curl near my left ear. The wedding dress was at least two sizes too big and hung limp on my frame. It looked ridiculous with my bright pink bra straps. I couldn't care less.

"Let's go," the men said as one of them grabbed me by the upper arm and dragged me from the room.

The moment I reentered the main church, my eyes searched for Brooklyn. A door opened and she appeared. I called out to her, "It's going to be okay."

She nodded as her eyes filled with tears.

Pavel stood by my side, swaying as he leaned on his cane. The priest appeared, to lead us to the center of the church.

My mouth twisted in a sneer. "You should be ashamed of yourself."

The priest cast his eyes down but refused to respond.

As Pavel moved forward, I couldn't make my feet move. A hand on my back shoved me so hard I stumbled a few steps and then slowly walked on. We reached the small platform, which was covered in rose-colored fabric we would stand on, symbolizing our new life together. I felt sick.

When it came to the part where I had to state that I was marrying of my own free will, my mouth went dry. I tried several times to form the words, but they wouldn't come. Then I heard a muffled scream from the side. One of the henchmen had wrapped his arm around Brooklyn's throat as he shoved a gun to her head. I spit the words out.

Two men held the wedding crowns over our heads.

Pavel stated, "I, Pavel Petrov, take you, Katia Novikova, as my wedded wife, and I promise you love, honor, and respect; to be faithful to you; and not to forsake you, until death do us part. So help me God, one in the Holy Trinity, and all the Saints."

I couldn't believe he was uttering such vile lies in a house of God.

The priest looked at me. I knew it was my turn. I knew once I uttered those words the priest would place the crowns on our heads and we would be considered married.

I looked over at Brooklyn who still had a gun pressed to her head.

The back double doors of the church slammed open.

Luka strolled in. "Her name is Katie. Now get your fucking hands off my girl."

CHAPTER 29

Luka

Our men swarmed in from all sides. The Novikoff and Petrov men guarding the doors were taken out first with quick shots to the head. Gregor, Damien, Mikhail, and I stormed down the aisle.

I pointed in Brooklyn's direction and called out to one of my men, "Save her!"

I knew Katie would never forgive me if I let her friend die.

As the Ivanovs battled Egor and Pavel's men, I headed straight for Katie. She was leaving here as my fiancée or as a widow, but either way she wasn't going to spend one goddamn minute married to another man. It would never have been our wish to shed blood in a church, but we hadn't chosen this battlefield. Her father had.

I would risk the damnation of God himself to rescue my girl.

I had failed her earlier. I would not fail her again.

Pavel Petrov blocked my path. "What is the meaning of this, Siderov?"

"She's mine, Petrov. Now get the fuck away from her."

"Over my dead body," Petrov threatened as he pushed Katie further behind him.

He was already a dead man, but the moment he touched her sealed his gruesome fate. I would enjoy killing him slowly, making sure his every plea for mercy fell on deaf ears.

"Your choice." I raised my gun and pointed it directly between his eyes. "Get away from her. Now."

Before I could even pull the trigger Pavel clutched his chest and fell backward. His head bounced off the tiles as he landed with a thud. I reached down and fisted his tie, lifting him up just high enough so he could hear me say, "We slaughtered your sons like the pigs they were. When you die, your seed dies with you."

His eyes widened. He tried clawing at my sleeve before his sightless eyes rolled back in his head. I dropped his lifeless body back to the floor and kicked him aside.

I locked eyes with Katie.

With an anguished cry, she started to fall to her knees. I caught her in my arms, crushing her slight form against my chest, whispering how much I loved and adored her in Russian against the top of her head over and over and over again. *"Ya tebya obozhayu. Ya tebya lyublyu. Ty moya dusha."*

I pulled back to inspect her for injuries. My jaw

clenched when I saw the bruise forming under her eye. "Point to the bastard who did that to you."

Katie pointed to one of the men who had attacked us earlier. I now knew his name was Nikolay.

The moment he laid eyes on me he tried to run. I chased him down and launched into his back, sending us both sprawling. I rolled him over and straddled him. Using the butt of my gun, I smashed his eye socket. "Let's see how you like it, asshole."

I hit him again and again.

It was only Katie's cry that broke through my fog. There would be plenty of time to kill this piece of shit. Right now she needed me. I stood up and gave Nikolay a kick in the ribs for good measure. I then motioned to one of my men. "Get this garbage out of my sight. Take him to the warehouse with the others who are still unlucky enough to be alive."

My man smirked. "Not for long they won't be."

I walked back to Katie and enfolded her in my arms, kissing her bruised cheek.

I leaned back and cupped her jaw. Staring deeply into her eyes, I vowed, "I will die before I let anything ever happen to you again, my love. Do you understand me? You are my life. My world. I will protect you with every drop of my blood."

Tears fell down her cheeks. "Don't say that! Don't say you'll die for me."

I kissed her forehead. "I am making this vow in a church before God. You are mine, Katie, and no one is ever going to separate me from you again."

She leaned back and clutched at my forearms. "Please

don't say such things. I thought you were dead. I couldn't bear it. I died with you in that moment. I'm so sorry."

My brow lowered. "You have nothing to apologize for. This was not your fault, babygirl. Evil men do evil things."

She shook her head as she caressed my cheek with her hand. "No. I'm sorry for not saying I love you back when I had a chance. I was too much in my head. Too worried it was too soon and a thousand other stupid things that don't matter now. I love you, Luka. I don't care if I've only known you for a short time. I don't care what that means for my future plans. I love you."

I cupped the back of her head and pulled her forward. My lips captured hers. I wanted to taste the sweet words on her lips. My tongue swept inside, claiming her as my own. We were both breathless when I broke free. I gripped her hair and tilted her head back, needing her beautiful gaze on mine. "I want you to listen very carefully, babygirl. Your future remains the same. You are going to graduate and open your business and become a famous photographer sought by collectors the world over. The only difference is that I will be by your side. *As your husband.*"

The tightness in my chest that started the moment I had woken up in the ambulance with her nowhere in sight only slightly eased. It wouldn't fully be gone until she bore my name and forever ditched the name Novikoff.

She leaned up on her toes and clutched at my shoulders to kiss me again.

The move opened my stitches, sending a trickle of fresh blood seeping through the bandages.

She covered her mouth with her hand. "Fuck! Your injury! Oh, my God! I've hurt you."

I pulled her close. "The only thing that could hurt me is not having you near."

"Katie!" called out Brooklyn as she made her way through the church pews toward us.

Katie tried again to pull away. My arms tightened. She raised her face with pleading eyes. It went against the grain to ever let her go again, but finally I relented.

Katie raced over to Brooklyn. My man stepped back as Katie embraced her. "I'm so sorry! I'm so sorry about everything! I'm so sorry this happened. I'm so sorry I lied to you. I'm a terrible, terrible friend!"

Brooklyn hugged her back. "I knew you couldn't be as boring as you pretended."

Katie leaned back. "So you're not mad at me?"

"Mad? I have a badass mafia princess for a friend who commands a freaking army of sexy, scary-as-hell Russian men. Hell, no. *Traumatized?* Yes. I don't think I'll be sleeping with the light off anytime soon."

I stood over both of them. Placing my hands on Katie's shoulders, I said to Brooklyn, "Anything you want or need is yours. I'll see you have round-the-clock guards until you feel safe again."

Brooklyn pointed to my man Andrei who was standing over her. "Can I have him?"

Andrei met my gaze and grinned. I winked at Brooklyn. "Consider it done."

Katie turned to face me. "My father! He was behind all of this. Did you… is he… dead?"

I shook my head no. "We saw him slink out a back

door the moment the fighting started. I gave word to our men to let him escape. I didn't know how you'd feel if we... well... if we killed him."

Her eyes narrowed. "His men shot and almost killed you. They kidnapped and terrorized my best friend. He almost forced me to marry that odious man. He also hurt my mother. He's no father to me. I want him dead, Luka. I want him dead so he can never be a threat to us again."

I nodded solemnly.

Gregor and Damien had approached us and overheard Katie's declaration.

Gregor raised his chin. "We'll take care of it."

Damien called out to Mikhail who was supervising the rounding up of the bodies. "Mikhail!"

Mikhail turned.

Damien continued. "Gloves off, brother. Go get the bastard."

Mikhail's lips lifted in a cold smile. "My pleasure."

No one survived the moment they were caught in the sights of Mikhail's sniper rifle. Her father would be dead before he hit the ground, probably within the hour. It was a long overdue payback for Egor's sons targeting his wife last year.

I bent low and swept Katie into my arms.

She protested. "Luka! Your shoulder."

I gave her a squeeze. "Hush. It's just a scratch. I need to get you out of here and out of that horrendous dress."

She wrinkled her nose. "It *is* terrible." She looked over her shoulder. "I need to take care of Brooklyn."

At that moment, Andrei lifted Brooklyn into his arms. I chuckled. "Your friend is fine."

As I walked her out of the church, she leaned her head on my good shoulder. "With my father and Petrov dead, I guess there is no more threat to me, which means *technically* we don't have to get married for my own protection now."

I lowered my head and growled in her ear, "Nice try, princess. I'm not that easy to get rid of."

CHAPTER 30

Katie

I OPENED my eyes the moment Luka carried me over the threshold of his hotel suite.

It felt like home.

He laid me gently on the bed. Lifting up my torso, he unzipped the heinous wedding gown and stripped it off my body. He then unhooked my bra and removed my panties. He wrapped me in the soft comforter as he stood and turned.

I reached out to grab his hand. "Where are you going?"

The trauma of the last few hours was starting to settle in. The idea of not having his strong presence by my side frightened me. I needed him to slay the demons that were lurking in the shadows, getting ready to pounce the moment there was silence.

He gripped my hand, leaned over, and kissed me on

the forehead. "I'm running you a bath. I'll only be a few feet away, baby."

He crossed from the bed into the bathroom. I heard the rush of water into the tub. Luka returned wearing only a hotel robe. I stretched my arms up and wrapped them around his neck. He carried me into the bathroom where a tub filled with silky bubbles waited. He lowered me down into the deep Jacuzzi-style tub.

His hands reached for his belt. As he shrugged off his robe, I grimaced at the ugly, thick black stitches on his shoulder and side now visible since he'd ripped off the gauze bandage.

He shrugged. "They're only scratches. It would take more than a few bullets to take me from you, baby."

I shook my head. "Still, should you be getting your stitches wet? Maybe you should keep the bandage on."

He smirked, "Fuck my stitches."

He stepped into the tub, his large body displacing the water and sending a wave of soapy bubbles onto the floor. He positioned himself behind me and placed me on his lap with my back nestled against his chest. I knew he was doing this so I wouldn't look at his stitches and get upset, and I loved him for it.

Luka poured a generous amount of liquid soap into a washcloth and ran it up and down my arms. I moaned as I leaned my head back onto his good shoulder. A few hours ago, I thought I'd never feel clean again. Now the warm water and the soft, floral scent of the soap soothed my body and soul. But the strong feel of Luka's arms around me was far from soothing. It aroused a need to feel his rough hands between my legs. I needed to feel him inside of me. It was as if that was the only way I would truly believe we were both alive and well.

I grabbed his wrist and moved his hand over my pussy.

Luka growled into my ear. "Are you sure?"

I shifted my hips, feeling the press of his hard cock. "I'm sure."

"You've been through a lot today and I have to be honest. I'm not sure I can be as gentle as you need me to be."

I shimmied my hips again. "Who says I want you to be gentle?"

Fuck gentle. That wasn't us. I needed him to grab me by the hips and pound into me so hard I forgot my own name. That was how I wanted to get past the trauma of today.

Luka chuckled. "God, I fucking love you."

He pressed two fingers deep inside of me as his thumb brushed my clit. His other hand caressed my breast as he pinched and teased my nipple.

I moaned again.

"You like that, baby?"

"Oh, fuck, yes."

He pinched my nipple just as he pinched my clit. Jesus, I was going to come already. There was just something about this man's hands. He thrust his fingers inside of me as I moved my hips. Reaching behind me, I stroked the thick, hard length of his cock, pressing it against my lower back as I moved in rhythm with his fingers.

I cried out my release and collapsed back against him.

Luka shifted his position and raised his leg. He used

his foot to press a button on the side of the Jacuzzi tub. "Now for the real fun."

He pushed his hips up and used his knees to open my legs wide just as the jets turned on.

A forceful stream of water hit my sensitive clit. "Oh! Oh! Oh, God!"

His hands cupped my ass. His fingers then caressed between my cheeks to tease my asshole.

I inhaled sharply as my bottom cheeks clenched. "Wait. I've never…"

Luka nipped at my ear. "Your last virgin hole. After tonight you are completely mine."

He pushed a finger in to the first knuckle, gently swirling it around. It felt strange and yet exciting. He thrust it in a little further and repeated the gesture several times. All the while, the jet from the Jacuzzi teased my clit.

Luka shifted as he reached for the liquid soap. I watched with trepidation as he slathered it over his fingers. I bit my lip as he once again used his hand to lift my hips. This time I felt two fingers tease my hole. I hissed through my teeth as the pressure increased.

"Easy, easy," he murmured against my neck as he pushed two fingers inside of me and twisted them back and forth, working the soap in deeper.

He pulled his fingers free. His knuckles brushed the under curve of my ass as he fisted his cock. He pressed the tip against me.

I gripped the edge of the tub. "Luka," I breathed.

Without allowing me to tense any further, he pushed the head of his cock into my ass.

I opened my mouth on a silent cry as my hips rose, trying to escape the pain. "Wait. You're too big. We can't."

"This is happening, princess."

He pushed in another inch.

My body struggled to accommodate him; I could feel the tight ring of muscle stretch around his length. My fingers slipped on the tub edge as I tried to lift my body up. Luka's large hands spanned my hips and pushed me back down, forcing another thick inch of his shaft inside of me.

"You're going to take every inch into that tight ass of yours."

He pushed his hips up, spearing me.

My legs kicked, splashing water as I held my breath, internalizing the pain and inexplicable pleasure.

"Keep your legs open, babygirl."

He pushed in another inch. I rotated my hips, trying to ease the intense pressure.

"Fuck!" growled Luka.

Like a monster rising from the depths of the ocean, Luka rose out of the tub, holding me before him. He placed my torso on the edge of the tub as he rose on his knees behind me. Now my pussy was pressed even closer to the Jacuzzi jet. The increased pressure of the water stream sent me over the edge. My orgasm sent a shockwave through my body.

As I tried to recover, I looked over my shoulder.

Luka held the bottle of liquid soap over my ass. He squeezed it, sending a cool stream of iridescent liquid soap pouring down my ass crack. He then settled one restraining hand on my lower back as he fisted his other in my hair. My back arched as this time he thrust deep inside my ass.

I screamed as my body absorbed the full impact of his thrust.

He thrust in again and again, showing no mercy as my body struggled to accept him. There was something just so dirty sexy wrong about allowing this beast of a man to fuck me up the ass and I loved every minute of it. I took the pain with the pleasure and leaned in, wanting to feel it all, every inch of him, as he ruthlessly claimed me.

"Who owns you, babygirl?"

I remembered him asking me that very same question the first time we had sex. I'd flippantly told him *no one owns me*. Now that wasn't even close to true. This man owned me body and soul. If he asked, I would get down on my knees and crawl through broken glass just to suck his cock. He had opened a whole world of pleasure to me, and I was going to relish every dirty touch, lick, and fuck.

"You do, baby. You do," I called out.

Luka spanked my wet ass. "Damn right I do."

CHAPTER 31

*L*uka

I REACHED over to accept the lighter from Gregor. I then leaned back and lit my cigar.

Gregor breathed a smoke ring into the air before asking, "Are you really going to wait three months to marry the girl?"

Damien shook his head. "You're a better man than me, my friend."

I looked out over the spacious, well-manicured lawn of Gregor's estate where we were relaxing on the flagstone back patio. The large pine trees obscured the sniper watchtowers and massive fence he used to protect his family. To the left was Damien's property and a little further down the street was Mikhail's. They had literally surrounded themselves with family.

I tossed the lighter on the table between us. "I want

what you have," I said, gesturing around me. "Property. Family. Roots. I also want to give that to Katie. After her mother passed, she was for all intents and purposes alone in the world, like me. We are going to be each other's family."

Vaska and Dimitri strolled out onto the patio from inside.

Vaska handed Damien a green glass bottle of Moskovskaya vodka, as he and Dimitri placed tall shot glasses on the table. "What are we, chopped liver?" complained Vaska.

Dimitri slapped me on the shoulder. "We are all your family now, Luka. Try and get rid of us."

For years, I had considered these men as friends and business associates but no more. I kept myself at a distance. Always on the outer edges of their lives. They called upon me when they needed a cold-blooded mercenary. A ruthless bastard with no ties or loyalty to any family to hold him down, but that was all over now. I wanted a life with Katie. I wanted to see her carrying my child. I wanted her to finally have a home, a place where she felt needed and loved and protected.

I exhaled a fragrant cloud of smoke as I reached for my shot glass. "You are correct. We are no longer friends. We are chosen brothers."

We all raised our glasses and kicked back the shot of vodka.

All of us, except Vaska, grimaced.

Damien tossed his glass down. "Jesus Christ, Vaska. You have the worst fucking taste in vodka."

Gregor held his hand to his throat. "I can feel it boring a hole through my insides."

Dimitri shrugged and poured another glass.

I stared at Dimitri in horror. "I've had better vodka from a toilet in a Siberian prison. How are you drinking this swill?"

Dimitri cast a hard glance over at Vaska. "You get used to it when *someone* gives you no other choice."

Vaska smirked. "You are all pussies. This is great stuff. The stuff of our people!"

Gregor shook his head. He then turned to me. "Did you get ahold of Maxim and Ivan?"

I nodded. "Yes, they will return to America in time for the wedding. Maxim plans to stay indefinitely. His bride, Carinna, wants to finish her degree. Ivan will return to Russia right after the wedding."

Damien rested his feet on a wicker ottoman. "Damn. I was hoping for his help brokering a new deal with the Saudi Arabians. They're flying in the week after the wedding to meet with me and Mikhail."

"You may convince him to stay for a little while longer, but his wife, Dylan, is pregnant and he wants his son born in Russia."

Gregor kicked his head back and laughed. "A son. Tell him good luck with that. So far it is only daughters from us."

Dimitri nodded in solidarity. "Soon we will have to build our own convent, since none of them will ever marry, of course."

Gregor waved his cigar hand in his direction and

nodded. "I will shoot any man who dares touch my little Sophia."

I took a long drag from my cigar and listened to them continue to casually chat about business, their wives, and future plans.

A feeling of contentment settled in my chest.

Life was good.

Life would be even better when Katie was finally my wife.

While I was impatiently waiting to make her so, I was occupying my time by building her a dream home only a mile down the road across from Mikhail and Nadia's property. It would have plenty of space and light, so she would feel the warmth of the sun no matter what room she entered.

Her life had been cold and lonely until now. I was going to fill it with warmth and love. I was also building her a state-of-the-art photographer's studio and darkroom. I couldn't wait to surprise her on our wedding day. Later today, I would be picking up a hand-carved wood and brass sign I had ordered to welcome everyone to our home. On the brass plate it read *Alina's Solace*, after Katie's mother. I thought she would like it.

It was nice worrying about what another person would or would not like, wondering what would please them and make them happy. I'd never had that in my life before. I couldn't wait to spoil my babygirl rotten. She would want for nothing. Never again would she feel unloved or alone. She would be surrounded by people who loved her, a chosen family of brothers and sisters.

And soon, if God was willing, we'd have a little son or

daughter for me to spoil as well. Never in my life would I have thought such domestic ideas would appeal to me. Now I couldn't imagine a day, an hour, even a minute without Katie's love.

Vaska interrupted my quiet thoughts when he stood and poured another round of shots.

We all groaned.

Vaska chastised us good-naturedly. "Shut up, you weaklings."

Resigned to our fate, we raised a second glass.

"To friendship," said Vaska.

"To brotherhood," I said.

Gregor smiled. "To family."

Damien winked. "To love."

Dimitri chimed in, "To our women!"

"To our women!" we all chanted before braving another shot of Vaska's favorite cheap-ass vodka.

Samara swung open the French glass doors behind us. She called over her shoulder, "They're hiding out on the patio!"

Damien sat up straighter. "Hardly hiding!"

Soon the patio was a hive of activity as Samara, Emma, Yelena, and Mary poured over the threshold.

Gregor reached to take baby Sophia from Samara's hands.

She swung the baby out of his reach and rested the little girl on her hip. "Cigar!"

Gregor rested his cigar in a nearby glass ashtray.

Samara's lips thinned. "Stub it out."

"*Malýshka*, it's a Cuban," complained Gregor.

Samara raised a single eyebrow.

With a resigned sigh, Gregor stubbed out the cigar while muttering something about getting his belt out later. Samara handed him his little girl. The baby fussed for a moment before settling down in the crook of his arm. Her big blue eyes stared up at him in wonder.

Emma handed Dimitri his little girl, Elizabeth. "Don't forget to read to her before you put her down for her nap. We are on chapter fifteen of *Pride and Prejudice*. I left the book by the cradle."

Dimitri stroked his hand down Emma's cheek as he settled his daughter on his shoulder. "*Moya kroshka*, she is just a baby. She cannot understand a word you are saying."

Emma raised her shoulder as one corner of her mouth lifted in a cheeky grin. "You don't know that."

Dimitri kissed her on the forehead. "Very well, love. I'll read to her."

She kissed him back on the cheek.

Yelena wrapped her arms around Damien's neck from behind. "We won't be long. We're taking Katie and Brooklyn out to dinner. I want them to meet Emma and Mary."

Damien lifted up her hand and kissed the inside of her wrist. "Take the bulletproof SUV, not the Range Rover, and tell Andrei he better have you all back and *reasonably* sober by midnight."

Mary picked up Vaska's bottle of Moskovskaya vodka. "I'd warn you five to stay sober as well, but I have a feeling that will not be a problem if this is the crap you're drinking."

Vaska gave her a playful swat on the ass before grabbing her around the waist and giving her a lusty kiss. "Keep up with that sassy mouth and you won't be going anywhere, you'll be too busy *tending to your husband's needs.*"

All the women laughed as they dragged Mary away from Vaska and back into the house.

The patio returned to a companionable silence.

Dimitri paced the length of it as he bounced his little girl on his shoulder while Gregor's baby fell asleep in his arms.

I leaned back and turned my attention to Damien. "Tell me about this Saudi Arabian deal."

Damien leaned in. "They want at least twenty-five cases of Steyr SSG-69, which isn't a problem. The issue is with the Sako TRG 42s they are requesting."

Yes. Life was good.

CHAPTER 32

Katie
Three months later

"Shhh... you'll wake her!" whispered Brooklyn.

A series of giggles followed.

I opened one eye, but then quickly shut it. I buried my head deeper into my pillow to hide my smile.

"Do you have the ties?"

"Where's the veil?"

"Who has the vodka?"

There was more scuffling and a muffled curse as someone must have bumped into the coffee table.

"This suite is so freaking small. How have they been living here for three months?"

I stifled a laugh.

Luka and I had been living out of his hotel suite for the last several months. After turning down all my suggestions for getting an apartment, I was finally able to work it out of him that he was building us a house. No, not a house, a home. The first home I would have since my mother died. It was supposed to be a surprise and still was since he refused to tell me any of the details, only that it was close to Nadia, Yelena, and Samara's homes, which was fabulous since we had all become close friends. He even promised there was room for Brooklyn to visit. Not that she would need it. In the months since her harrowing introduction into my family's mafia life, she and Andrei had become inseparable. While she thought I was crazy for marrying Luka so young, I had a feeling she wasn't going to be that far behind me.

In the meantime, we continued to work on our plans for a business together. Recently the plans had expanded to include the other girls as well. The boys had found an old warehouse close to downtown Alexandria. It was an historic building from the colonial era with beautiful exposed brick and gorgeous thick wooden beams. We dreamed of turning it into a big artists' studio where customers could come to buy my photographs, Samara's paintings, Brooklyn's sculptures, Yelena's fashions, and Nadia's jewelry. It was going to be perfect.

I couldn't believe that in the span of a few months I had gone from a cloistered life where I had no true family who cared about me, barely even letting my own best friend in, to having a whole new band of sisters.

And it was all because of that stubborn, arrogant, pain-in-the-ass, gorilla of a man who I loved more than life itself. I thought of the carefully wrapped book that was hidden in my underwear drawer. It was a present for Luka for our wedding day. I had found an original copy of

The Old Man and the Sea. I couldn't wait to give it to him. I couldn't wait to get married to him! I couldn't wait to start our life together. There was so much to look forward to.

Brooklyn whispered again, "So, are we supposed to tie her up?"

Yelena answered, "Only if she gives us trouble."

I could tell they had surrounded my bed.

Just then, Mary burst through the bedroom door. "Surprise!"

"Mary!" they all shouted at once. "You woke her up!"

I sprang up, no longer able to pretend I was asleep. "What's going on here?" I asked, playing along.

Brooklyn jumped up and down. "We're kidnapping you for ransom!"

Since dating Andrei, Brooklyn had embraced all things Russian, including the wedding tradition of kidnapping the bride for ransom. The tradition was to kidnap the bride, usually on the day of her wedding, but thankfully I was actually getting married tomorrow. The bride was then *ransomed* to the groom who had to beat numerous obstacles to win back her return, including bribing her friends with jewelry and alcohol.

It was strange to think of the lengths to which I had gone to avoid everything about my heritage, even to the point of lying about my real name. And now none of that seemed to matter. Now, thinking about these customs and traditions didn't bring shame or fear, only love and companionship and, finally, a true sense of family.

I jumped out of the bed and ran out of the room. "Oh, no, you don't! I've had enough kidnapping for one life!"

Yelena called out, "Get her!"

Brooklyn blocked the exit to the hotel room. "You're not escaping that easily!"

Mary nodded to Emma. "You flank left, I'll go right."

Emma and Mary circled around me. They both held silk scarves between their hands.

I pointed to them both. "Don't you dare!"

I didn't see Samara and Nadia until it was too late.

Nadia grabbed me from behind, pinning my arms down. Mary lurched forward and loosely 'tied' my wrists together as Samara placed a voluminous white wedding veil on my head.

Yelena started to chant as the others joined in. "Shots! Shots! Shots!"

I laughed. "Shots? It's eight in the morning!"

Emma wagged her finger at me. "No sass from the captive!"

I cupped the shot of vodka between my tied-up hands and kicked it back.

Everyone cheered.

Brooklyn stepped up close and pulled the white gauze over my face. "Now you must come with us!"

I tried to blow the veil away from my mouth. "Where are you taking me?"

"Wouldn't you like to know," teased Samara.

"Wait! I'm still in my pajamas!"

"Too bad!" laughed Mary.

They marched me out of the hotel room and down the hallway. Through the thin gauze I could see several of our usual bodyguards smiling and waving as we passed.

Playing along, I called out to them to rescue me. All my cries were ignored.

We piled into the back of a massive limousine.

Brooklyn held a shot up to me under my veil, which they wouldn't let me lift up. I kicked it back, already getting a fun, tipsy feeling.

After about twenty minutes we arrived at our destination. As Emma helped me out of the limousine, the familiar facade of our future business appeared as if through a mist as I stared out through the white gauze.

I was ushered through the door.

The girls then lifted my veil with a flourish.

I let out a shocked gasp.

The empty warehouse floor had been swept and cleaned. Massive bouquets of pink and white peonies burst from large clear glass vases arranged around the space on black marble pedestals. In the center of the room was a large, polished conference table covered in a white lace cloth. Sterling silver platters and three-tiered serving trays brimmed with caviar, lobster, artisan cheeses and meats, as well as cakes and sweets. In the center was a sterling silver swan, a Russian symbol of matrimonial love, about two feet tall and surrounded by more peonies in the center of the table. There was even the traditional, elegantly decorated *kournik* pies artfully arranged among the platters.

Brooklyn hugged me from behind. "What do you think?"

I leaned my head back on her shoulder. "This is definitely my best kidnapping yet."

A string quartet played in a corner as we laughed and sang and ate and drank.

Then suddenly, the front windows were smashed as several objects came flying through.

We all screamed and backed up.

Several small black, grenade-looking objects rolled across the floor, then burst open in a cloud of smoke... and silver glitter.

As the smoke cleared, we watched with anticipation as our men, dressed in full black fatigues, stalked in through the smashed windows.

Luka stepped forward out of the pack. "I'm here to claim my woman!"

Mary snatched me by the shoulders and led me around to the other side of the buffet table. "You'll have to fight us for her!"

Luka cast a glance to his right and left. "Men?"

Each of the men reached for their belts.

I covered my mouth as I screamed with laughter.

They held their belts between their hands and snapped the leather. The sound echoed around the cavernous room, even above the music.

As they slowly approached, we dumped the silver trays of sweets and held them up as shields. Each of us picked up a cupcake, top-heavy with icing.

Yelena called out in warning, "Not one more step, gentlemen!"

Damien laughed. "Be careful of my woman, men. I know from personal experience she has great aim."

Vaska joined in. "Unfortunately, so does mine," he said

as he nodded in Mary's direction as she lifted two cupcakes with each hand.

Luka shook his head. "They've left us no choice."

We each cast glances at one another, waiting for their next move. They slowly reached into their pants pockets and pulled out long strands of diamonds and pearls. As we exclaimed in glee, they tossed the precious jewelry onto the table.

Mary dropped her cupcake weapons as she picked up a strand of diamonds. "Your ransom is accepted. Claim your bride!"

I cried out with shocked glee as Luka vaulted over the buffet table and snatched me around the waist. Before I knew what was happening, he swung me up into his arms.

Luka growled, "You're mine now, babygirl."

As he swept down to claim a kiss, I placed the cupcake with its sweet buttercream icing between us. "Tell me you love me first." Ever since he said it that first time, I never tired of hearing it. I was like someone starved for light now thrust into the sunshine.

Luka opened his mouth and took a large bite of mostly icing. He swallowed and slowly licked his lips before lustily saying, "I love you, babygirl. Now and for always."

I wrapped my arms around his neck and kissed him, knowing life from this point forward would be as sweet as that kiss.

CHAPTER 33

Katie
The Wedding

I STARED at my reflection in the slightly chipped oval mirror.

My lower lip trembled as I smoothed the soft silk of my wedding gown over my hips.

I miss my mom.
I wish she could be here right now.

My eyes teared up. I pressed the knuckle of my forefinger against my lower lashes so the tears wouldn't ruin my makeup.

Just then the small side door to the bridal dressing chamber of the church swung open.

All the girls burst through in a chaotic flurry of silk, perfume, and chatter.

Mary tossed over her shoulder as she crossed the

threshold first, "You need to stop fussing with that damn wedding gown, Yelena. It's perfect."

Yelena countered, "I just want to make sure that lower seam on the right isn't buckling again."

Emma chimed in, "Did the boys make sure the crowns were placed on the altar?"

Samara answered. "Yes, that was Gregor's job."

Nadia giggled. "I'm making Mikhail steam the rose fabric over the center dais since it was looking a little wrinkled."

Brooklyn laughed as she carefully unwrapped my wedding bouquet from the florist box she held. "Bet he loved that!"

Carinna strolled in, arm in arm with Dylan. "You should have seen Maxim's face when I told him he was in charge of getting the wedding cake I made to the reception hall. I swear to God, there are like eight of his men helping him transport that thing. They are treating it like it's a bomb about to go off."

Dylan tousled Carinna's curls. "That's because he knows you'll become an unstable bomb if so much as one rose is smooshed on that four-tier masterpiece."

All laughter stopped the moment they spotted me.

I turned away as I tried to hide a sniffle and wipe my eyes.

"Oh, my God!"

"What's wrong?"

"Don't cry, sweetie!"

"Are you okay?"

I was immediately surrounded and embraced by all of them.

I sniffed again. "I'm fine! Really."

Brooklyn's eyes narrowed. "Did someone do or say something to upset you? I'll slice their throats."

Ever since becoming, as she called it, a mafia chick, Brooklyn had embraced some rather colorfully violent language.

I lowered my head as I wiped another tear. "No. It's silly. It's just… I wish my mom was here."

Once again, I was wrapped in their warm, perfumed embrace.

"Aw!"

"Sweetie!"

"It's not silly!"

"You poor thing!"

"I'm getting Luka."

I reached out. "No. I don't want to bother him."

Brooklyn refused to listen as she made a beeline for the door.

Samara took my hands as Yelena rubbed soothing circles on my back. "We could never replace your mom and I know you haven't known us for very long, but we truly consider you a sister. You're family now."

Yelena concurred. "We are going to be each other's mother and sister and aunt and friend. If you think about it, most of us are just a bunch of motherless souls."

I hadn't thought about that, but it was true. Many of the girls had either lost their mother at a young age like Yelena and Dylan or were estranged from them like Carinna. In a way, we really had chosen each other to create our own big family.

I lifted my head higher as I smiled.

Emma patted my shoulder. "Feel better?"

I nodded.

Yelena pushed everyone away from me. "Good. Now get back, you're crushing her gown."

Brooklyn came running back into the room. She was quickly followed by Luka.

Looking magnificent in a custom Armani tuxedo, his hard gaze zeroed in on me the moment he entered the room. He barreled through the women and wrapped his arms around my waist. His brow furrowed as he stared down at me. "What's the matter, babygirl? Are you okay? Did someone hurt you?"

I clutched at his strong arms. "No, I—"

Before I could finish, the rest of the men stormed into the room.

All with guns drawn.

Vaska demanded, "What's wrong?"

Gregor surveyed the room. "Where's the threat?"

Maxim crossed to Carinna. "Is everyone okay?"

Dimitri grabbed Emma and shoved her behind him as he raised his gun higher. "Stay behind me, baby."

Ivan snatched Dylan to his side. "We need to alert the men to secure the perimeter immediately."

Mikhail spoke into his cell phone as he reached for Nadia. "Have them bring the armored car around back. We need to get the girls out of here."

Damien stayed close to the threshold, guarding the door. "Yelena, stay down."

All the women's heads turned to stare aghast at Brooklyn.

She wrinkled her nose. "I may have given Luka the wrong impression."

Luka spoke through clenched teeth. "You said *come quickly*, Katie's in *trouble*."

Carinna stepped forward. "Yeah, well, in her defense, in the *normal* world that means she stubbed her toe or tore her hem."

Dylan crossed to stand near Carinna. She raised her chin. "It's not our fault that in your fucked-up world that means some rival criminal gang has tried to kidnap one of us… again!"

Emma snuck out from behind Dimitri's protective body to stand near the rest of the girls. "She has a point."

Vaska let out a frustrated sigh as he put his gun away. "Give up, men, we're outflanked."

Gregor gestured to all the women. "I'm not sure I like this at all. They're ganging up on us. How are we ever going to win an argument again?"

Damien tapped his belt buckle and winked. "The old-fashioned way."

All of us girls let out a shocked gasp as a guilty blush crept over our cheeks.

Mary threw her arms up into the air. "Okay, show's over, everyone. Let's give these two crazy kids a moment alone."

Brooklyn raced over and kissed me on the cheek. She then turned to Luka. "Sorry!"

He gave her a playful growl. "You will be when I tell Andrei about this."

Brooklyn blushed even hotter before piling out of the room with the rest of the group.

Luka waited until they closed the door behind them. He stepped closer and placed a hand under my chin. "The truth, princess. Why were you crying?"

"I wasn't crying."

His eyes narrowed. "Don't test me. I won't hesitate to flip that wedding gown over your head and spank that cute ass of yours until I get an answer."

"You wouldn't dare! Yelena would murder you if you wrinkled this gown."

"I'll risk it."

I laughed but still a tear fell down my cheek.

Luka brushed it away with his thumb as he cupped my cheek. "Please tell me, have you changed your mind about marrying me?"

"God, no! I love you!"

His large body visibly relaxed. "That's good. I'm not sure what the priest would have said if I were forced to carry you down the aisle over my shoulder."

I played with the small black diamond buttons on his dress shirt. "I was just missing my mom. I'm not sure she'd approve of me marrying back into the life."

"Would she have approved of you marrying a man who loves you more than life itself? Who'd do anything to see you safe, protected, and happy?" Luka leaned down and kissed my cheek. "I think she'd be happy you found someone who has every intention of making her daughter the center of his world." He kissed the corner of my lips. "Someone who will love and cherish you every moment there is breath in his body."

Luka always knew just the right thing to say to make everything all better.

I traced my lips over his as I teased, "You know, for a big, arrogant gorilla you can be quite poetic with your words."

He licked my bottom lip with the tip of his tongue. "You should see how *poetic* I can get with my tongue."

Luka walked forward, pushing me back against the wall as his large hands began to slowly draw my gown up over my hips.

The door burst open.

Yelena stood there with her hands on her hips. "Don't you dare wrinkle that gown!"

Brooklyn shook her head. "Really, you two? In a freaking church?"

Samara tapped her wrist. "The priest is waiting. Can you at least get married before you consummate the wedding?"

Luka pressed his forehead to mine. "What do you say, princess? Ready to become my queen?"

I slipped past him as I hiked up my gown. I sent him a cheeky wink over my shoulder as I headed toward the door that would lead to the church. "You'll have to catch me first."

I heard Luka's playful roar right before he was hard on my heels, as we both raced toward our future together.

THE END.

ABOUT THE AUTHOR

USA TODAY Bestselling Author in Dark Romance
She delights in writing Dark Romance books filled with
overly-possessive Billionaires, Taboo scenes and
Unexpected twists. She usually spends her ill-gotten gains
on martinis, travel and red lipstick. Since she can barely
boil water, she's lucky enough to be married to a sexy
Chef.

ALSO BY ZOE BLAKE

RUTHLESS OBSESSION SERIES

A Dark Mafia Romance

Sweet Cruelty

Dimitri & Emma's story

It was an innocent mistake.

She knocked on the wrong door.

Mine.

If I were a better man, I would've just let her go.

But I'm not.

I'm a cruel bastard.

I ruthlessly claimed her virtue for my own.

It should have been enough.

But it wasn't.

I needed more.

Craved it.

She became my obsession.

Her sweetness and purity taunted my dark soul.

The need to possess her nearly drove me mad.

A Russian arms dealer had no business pursuing a naive librarian student.

She didn't belong in my world.

I would bring her only pain.

But it was too late…

She was mine and I was keeping her.

Sweet Depravity

Vaska & Mary's story

The moment she opened those gorgeous red lips to tell me no, she was mine.

I was a powerful Russian arms dealer and she was an innocent schoolteacher.

If she had a choice, she'd run as far away from me as possible.

Unfortunately for her, I wasn't giving her one.

I wasn't just going to take her; I was going to take over her entire world.

Where she lived.

What she ate.

Where she worked.

All would be under my control.

Call it obsession.

Call it depravity.

I don't give a damn… as long as you call her mine.

Sweet Savagery

Ivan & Dylan's Story

I was a savage bent on claiming her as punishment for her family's mistakes.

As a powerful Russian Arms dealer, no one steals from me and gets away with it.

She was an innocent pawn in a dangerous game.

She had no idea the package her uncle sent her from Russia contained my stolen money.

If I were a good man, I would let her return the money and leave.

If I were a gentleman, I might even let her keep some of it just for frightening her.

As I stared down at the beautiful living doll stretched out before me like a virgin sacrifice,

I thanked God for every sin and misdeed that had blackened my cold heart.

I was not a good man.

I sure as hell wasn't a gentleman… and I had no intention of letting her go.

She was mine now.

And no one takes what's mine.

Sweet Brutality

Maxim & Carinna's story

The more she fights me, the more I want her.

It's that beautiful, sassy mouth of hers.

It makes me want to push her to her knees and dominate her, like the brutal savage I am.

As a Russian Arms dealer, I should not be ruthlessly pursuing an innocent college student like her, but that would not stop me.

A twist of fate may have brought us together, but it is my twisted obsession that will hold her captive as my own treasured possession.

She is mine now.

I dare you to try and take her from me.

Sweet Ferocity

Luka & Katie's Story

I was a mafia mercenary only hired to find her, but now I'm going to keep her.

She is a Russian mafia princess, kidnapped to be used as a pawn in a dangerous territory war.

Saving her was my job. Keeping her safe had become my obsession.

Every move she makes, I am in the shadows, watching.

I was like a feral animal: cruel, violent, and selfishly out for my own needs. Until her.

Now, I will make her mine by any means necessary.

I am her protector, but no one is going to protect her from me.

IVANOV CRIME FAMILY TRILOGY

A Dark Mafia Romance

Savage Vow

Gregor & Samara's story

I took her innocence as payment.

She was far too young and naïve to be betrothed to a monster like me.

I would bring only pain and darkness into her sheltered world.

That's why she ran.

I should've just let her go…

She never asked to marry into a powerful Russian mafia family.

None of this was her choice.

Unfortunately for her, I don't care.

I own her… and after three years of searching… I've found her.

My runaway bride was about to learn disobedience has consequences… punishing ones.

Having her in my arms and under my control had become an obsession.

Nothing was going to keep me from claiming her before the eyes of God and man.

She's finally mine… and I'm never letting her go.

Vicious Oath

Damien & Yelena's story

When I give an order, I expect it to be obeyed.

She's too smart for her own good, and it's going to get her killed.

Against my better judgement, I put her under the protection of my powerful Russian mafia family.

So imagine my anger when the little minx ran.

For three long years I've been on her trail, always one step behind.

Finding and claiming her had become an obsession.

It was getting harder to rein in my driving need to possess her… to own her.

But now the chase is over.

I've found her.

Soon she will be mine.

And I plan to make it official, even if I have to drag her kicking and screaming to the altar.

This time… there will be no escape from me.

Betrayed Honor

Mikhail & Nadia's story

Her innocence was going to get her killed.

That was if I didn't get to her first.

She's the protected little sister of the powerful Ivanov Russian mafia family - the very definition of forbidden.

It's always been my job, as their Head of Security, to watch over her but never to touch.

That ends today.

She disobeyed me and put herself in danger.

It was time to take her in hand.

I'm the only one who can save her and I will fight anyone who tries to stop me, including her brothers.

Honor and loyalty be damned.

She's mine now.

For a list of All of Zoe Blake's Books Visit her Website!

www.zblakebooks.com

Printed in Great Britain
by Amazon